SUNDANCE #41

THE CAGE

Peter McCurtin

LEISURE BOOKS ☮ NEW YORK CITY

A LEISURE BOOK

Published by

Nordon Publications, Inc.
Two Park Avenue
New York, N.Y. 10016

Copyright © 1982 by Nordon Publications, Inc.

All rights reserved
Printed in the United States

THE LAW AND THE OUTLAW

Bracken put his foot on a rock and leaned forward on his knee. "There's more than just doing your time. This is no Eastern jail where you sit in your cell twenty hours a day and sew mailbags. There you can keep out of trouble if you try hard. Here it's different. What has the Actor told you about me? You won't be telling tales out of school. The Actor talks about everybody."

"He says you're a very tough man. Blaisdell runs the prison and you run the prisoners."

Bracken chewed his grizzled mustache. Mustaches were against the rules, but he had one, and it looked like he got to shave every day. His hair, no prison clip, was clean and combed.

"The Actor said right," Bracken said. "Could be that I'll have use for a man of your talents. You've done what couldn't be done, eh?" He lowered his voice. "You think you could break out of here?"

"There's nothing can't be done," Sundance answered. "It just has to be figured out."

Bracken took his foot off the rock and lit another cheroot. His pocket bulged with cheroots. His eyes narrowed. "You think I haven't tried to figure a way out?" The question didn't seem to demand an answer. "I'll have to think about you, Sundance. Maybe you won't have to stay on this rockpile for long. There are other jobs that don't break a man's back. Like I say, I'll have to think about it."

We will send you a free catalog on request. Any titles not in your local bookstore can be purchased by mail. Send the price of the book plus 50¢ shipping charge to Leisure Books, P.O. Box 511, Murray Hill Station, New York, N.Y. 10156-0511.

Titles currently in print are available for industrial and sales promotion at reduced rates. Address inquiries to Nordon Publications, Inc., Two Park Avenue, New York, N.Y. 10016, Attention: Premium Sales Department.

The SUNDANCE Series

No. 1	Overkill	No. 22	Ride the Man Down
No. 2	Dead Man's Canyon	No. 23	Gunbelt
No. 3	Dakota Territory	No. 24	Canyon Kill
No. 4	Death in Lava	No. 25	Blood Knife
No. 5	The Pistoleros	No. 26	The Nightriders
No. 6	The Bronco Trail	No. 27	Death Dance
No. 7	The Wild Stallions	No. 28	The Savage
No. 8	Bring Me His Scalp	No. 29	Day of the Halfbreeds
No. 9	Taps at Little Big Horn	No. 30	Los Olvidados
No. 10	The Ghost Dancers	No. 31	The Marauders
No. 11	The Comancheros	No. 32	Scorpion
No. 12	Renegade	No. 33	Hangman's Knot
No. 13	Honcho	No. 34	Apache War
No. 14	War Party	No. 35	Gold Strike
No. 15	Bounty Killer	No. 36	Trail Drive
No. 16	Run for Cover	No. 37	Iron Men
No. 17	Manhunt	No. 38	Drumfire
No. 18	Blood on the Prairie	No. 39	Buffalo War
No. 19	War Trail	No. 40	The Hunters
No. 20	Riding Shotgun	No. 41	The Cage
No. 21	Silent Enemy		

Chapter One

SUNDANCE smiled when he saw the flash of field-glasses high up on the mountain. It was hard to sneak up on Crook; the old soldier never missed a thing. It was a sunny day in late spring and the upland meadows were carpeted with flowers.

Mounted on the great stallion Eagle, he began the long climb to the hunting lodge, a big log building that stood on a wide step in the side of the mountain. Sundance knew it well; he had helped to build it, and he had been there many times since then, to hunt and fish with his old friend. He was glad to be back, but he sensed that Crook's one-sentence telegraph message—COME TO COLORADO—had nothing to do with game or fish.

General Crook loved the lodge and the Colorado mountains. Only there could he get away from the grind of army life, the never-ending Indian wars, the military politicking he hated so much. A simple man in spite of his great abilities, Crook always lamented the fact that he hadn't been born fifty years earlier. He should have been an old-fashioned mountain man, he said. A few weeks in the mountains, now and then, were as close as he got.

"Hello the house," Sundance shouted when he

reached the top of the ridge.

Crook shouted back from inside the house. "Fish on the fire, Jim. Got to watch it doesn't burn. Come on in."

Sundance unsaddled Eagle and turned him loose to graze on the sweet green grass not yet burned by the summer sun. Good cooking smells came from the house. Sundance went in.

Crook was busy with a panful of rainbow trout. "I spotted you a long way off," he said.

"I spotted you too, Three Stars," Sundance said, smiling. "Three Stars" was the name by which Crook was known to the Indians. Sundance never called him anything else. He was a three-star general in the Army of the United States, hence the name.

Sundance looked at the many big game trophies that decorated the rough pine walls of the lodge. "That bighorn head looks new," he said.

"Shot it last fall," Crook said.

Up so high, the wind was cold, whistling in the branches of trees that grew close to the house. Crook turned the fish in the pan. "You've been in Mexico, so you can't have known that Selden Myler is in prison. The charge was murder, the sentence was life."

Crook slid the fish onto a serving platter and put it on the table. "I was just as surprised," he said. "Obviously a trumped-up charge, yet three men swore that Myler shot an unarmed man in a poker game."

"Where?"

"Merced City, a small place just off the reservation. Myler was Indian agent at San Sebastian for umpteen years. You never went to see him there?"

"Never got around to it," Sundance answered. "No trouble, no need for me to go there. The last time I saw

Myler was about twelve years ago. That was when he saved my life. I haven't seen him since. They say he was doing a fine job at San Sebastian.''

Crook put the coffee pot on the table after dusting off the ashes from the fire. "Myler did too good a job. That's why he's in jail. He got a fair trial, it appears. Three men said he did it; there was only his word that he didn't. To boil it down: Myler was playing poker with four men in the back room of a saloon. Myler was winning big when the man who was killed accused him of cheating. There was some sort of scuffle and Myler was felled by a blow from behind. He says he heard two shots as he fell to the floor. When he came to, the sheriff was standing over him with Myler's pistol in his hand. Two bullets had been fired from it; there were two bullets in the dead man. The other men swore the dead man hadn't been armed. Maybe he wasn't. Anyway, no gun was found on the body. Either he wasn't armed or they took his gun and hid it after he was killed.''

"It sounds well thought-out," Sundance said.

"Pretty near fool-proof," Crook agreed. "Myler had a good lawyer, but he wasn't able to shake the witnesses. He checked their backgrounds as best he could, to see if they were connected in any way. It appeared not. The jury voted to convict. The judge could have sentenced Myler to hang. Instead, he gave him life imprisonment."

"What's the judge like?"

There was nothing to go with the fish, but there was plenty of fish. "You mean is the judge honest?" Crook said. "Honest enough, I guess. They tell me Judge Gans is a politician. Most judges are. What's the difference how honest he is? The verdict spoke for itself."

"Did the sheriff find any hold-out cards on Myler?"

"What do you think? Of course he did. I told you it was well planned."

"What do you know about the prosecutor?"

"Honest as they come, from what I hear. A man without mercy, though. Van Patten is his name and my information is he'd send his own mother to jail if she broke the law. This Van Patten demanded the death penalty for Myler. It must have been a disappointment when he didn't get his wish. What he got was the next best thing—life at hard labor. They might as well have hanged Myler. Myler hasn't been a well man these past few years. I doubt that he'd even survive an ordinary prison. In the Cage he'll be lucky if he lasts six months."

"They sent him to the Cage?"

The Cage—officially Sanderson Penitentiary—was notorious as the most brutal prison in the Southwest. It was wore than Yuma, in Arizona. It was worse than the worst prison camps in Arkansas or Mississippi.

"That's where they sent him," Crook said. "They could have sent him to the other prison in Fairfax. They sent him to the Cage. That's where they send the murderers, train robbers, rapists, perverts, the criminal lunatics. The bad boys."

Sundance was complying with Crook's directive to "eat hearty." All that morning, in the cold mountain wind, he had been thinking about good black coffee.

"Sending Myler to the Cage makes me wonder about the judge," Sundance said. "Why did the Indian Ring go to so much trouble to rig a murder charge? Why didn't they just kill Myler and blame it on the man he's supposed to have killed? Why didn't the judge sentence him to hang?"

"Three questions but only one answer," Crook said. "They wanted Myler to go to the Cage. It has to be that. Last year, Myler testified at the trial of the man—Ned Casserly—who had been his assistant. Myler brought the charges himself. He accused Casserly of selling thirty thousand dollars' worth of Indian supplies to merchants in towns close to the reservation. Casserly denied everything but was convicted—thank goodness for small mercies—and sent to jail for a year, a light sentence when you consider how much he stole. He got out and received a full pardon after serving only three months. It pays to be well-connected. I think Casserly and his cronies framed Myler into jail."

"It fits," Sundance said. "Everything fits. I can see a thief sitting in his cell plotting the destruction of an honest man."

Crook helped himself to more fish. "How much do you know about the Cage, Jim?"

"Just that it's a hellhole. I don't know that part of the territory. I've heard that men have killed themselves rather than go to the Sanderson pen."

"You heard right," Crook said. "It's living death there. That jail is a disgrace to this or any other country. I suppose Andersonville was worse, and the Union prison camp in Rock Island wasn't much better. But terrible things happen in a war. At least Andersonville and Rock Island weren't planned. The Cage was meant to be what it is. Another prison was needed in the territory. The other one dates back to Mexican times and isn't too secure, but there was no need to plan something like the Cage—not that I have much sympathy for men who commit violent crimes. Short of hanging them, which is what they ought to do, murderers and violent criminals should be locked up for life. No parole, no wangling of pardons. A lifetime in prison ought to be punishment enough. I just don't see the need to torment prisoners till their dying day."

"Who's the commandant there?" Sundance asked.

"It's not a military prison, Jim," Crook said. "The man in charge has the title of 'superintendent.' But you're not far off the mark. Blaisdell, the superintendent, was an army man at once time. Provost Marshal's department. Army police. Blaisdell was invalided out fifteen years ago and superintendent of the Cage is the only job he's had besides the army. Never married. Hardly ever leaves the damn place. That's all I know about him."

"You haven't tried to get Myler out?"

Crook frowned. "Get him out—how?"

"A pardon."

"Not a chance," Crook said. "If he worked for the Ring, like Casserly, he'd be out in no time. I just don't have that kind of pull. The fact is, it might make it worse for Myler if I started writing letters to Washington. Right now, Washington is a cesspool of corruption and double-dealing. As you know all too well. The President may be an honest man, but he can't see the forest for the crooks. The man is knee-deep in crooks and doesn't seem to know it. If the Ring thought I was trying to win a pardon for Myler, he'd be dead in a matter of days. Anyway, weeks. I think they're going to get Myler killed when they decide he's been in purgatory long enough. They may let him rot for a spell, but they'll kill him in the end. Word will come down from the Ring and Myler will be dead, that is, if disease or abuse don't kill him first."

Crook removed the fish bones and came back to the table with a large can of peaches. After hacking at it for a while he handed it to Sundance. "See what you can do with it."

Sundance got the can open. "What do you want me to do about Myler?" he asked.

"I don't know, Jim. I wanted you to know about it. You don't especially like Myler, do you? That's why you never went to see him?"

Sundance spooned out the peaches. "Myler saved my life. You know the story."

"I know he saved your life up on the Pecos. That's not what I asked you."

Sundance said, "Myler's a good man, but his attitude toward the Indians always got my back up. He used to call them 'my children,' like a Boston missionary. He liked to think of himself as a wise but stern father. He treated his 'children' well, but still as children. In Myler's view, the Indians didn't have the intelligence to stand on their own two feet. Myler's idea was to establish model reservations where the Indians ate well, had medical care, and could sing and dance to their hearts' content. We had plenty of arguments about that."

Crook smiled at this uncharacteristic outburst from Sundance, a man who displayed little emotion. "Still you have to admit it's better to have a man like Myler than one who will steal the Indians blind. How many times have I heard you go on about the rotten conditions on the reservations? The children with rickets or consumption. The rancid meat, the flimsy blankets, the women poxed up by white men, the men rotted with poisonous whiskey. How many times, Jim?"

"Too many times, Three Stars. You're right. Myler is a good man and I'm just nit-picking. You haven't said what you want me to do."

Crook finished his dessert and lit one of his long thin

cigars. He blew smoke at the ceiling. "Get him out if you can," he said. "If you think you can do it, if you want to do it. It may not be possible, even for you. Yes, I know everything is possible, or so they say. Jesus walked on water, but as some blasphemer once said, 'He couldn't have done it if he hadn't had such big feet.'"

"I'll get him out," Sundance said. "I'll do my best."

"Because he saved your life? I can't think of a better reason."

"I owe him that," Sundance said. "More important is the way he treated the Indians. He's given the best part of his life to his work, and I won't let the grafters grind him into the dirt."

A rockchuck came to the door and Crook got a biscuit from a box and tossed it to the twittering creature. "Be off, you thieving rodent," he said. The rockchuck nibbled at the biscuit and twittered back at him.

Crook said, "If you do get Myler out, what then? You may never get the truth of what happened, no matter how hard you try. The witnesses may be scattered far and wide by now. They may be dead. The Ring doesn't like loose ends."

"First thing is to get him out," Sundance said. "Then get him to Mexico. After that, I'll start digging for the truth. As you say, I may not find it. If I don't, Myler will have to stay in Mexico for the rest of his life. He won't like that. It's better than the Cage."

"Anything is better than the Cage," Crook said, tossing another hard biscuit to the chuck. "I wish I could do more to help you, Jim. Right now all I can do is give you the information I have. If it's money you need, I have a little and can get some more."

Sundance knew all about Crook's poor relatives, always begging for money and never refused. For all his gruffness, the old soldier was an easy touch.

"I made some money in Mexico," Sundance said. "The mine owner I chased the bandits for paid me well."

Crook put a match to another good cigar, his only indulgence. "I don't have to remind you we could go to jail just for having this conversation. What would the charge be, I wonder?"

"Conspiracy to violate the laws of the Territory of New Mexico. If you go to jail, I'll send you a file in a cake."

Crook returned Sundance's smile. "I don't like cake. The hell of it is, I'm a firm believer in the law. On the other hand, the law isn't set in concrete, and there are times when it has to be guided toward a right decision. Is that unconstitutional?"

"Probably," Sundance said. "I don't want you getting mixed up in this, Three Stars."

"Blast it, man. I *am* mixed up in it!"

Sundance shook his head. "You have too much to lose." He held up his hand to forestall Crook's angry denial. "You've been telling me what to do for a lot of years, and I'm grateful for most of it. Now I'm telling *you* what to do, with your permission, of course."

Crook scowled his way into a smile. "Permission granted."

"Stay out of this," Sundance went on. "I'm here for a visit, you didn't send me any message. I happened by and you told me Selden Myler was in prison, and for what. That's it, Three Stars. What happens after this has nothing to do with you. Is that clear, sir?"

Crook bit hard on his cigar. "No. It isn't."

"Sure it is," Sundance said. "You know nothing of

any plan to break Myler out of Sanderson jail. As far as you're concerned, Selden Myler is a convicted murderer who got what he deserved."

"Like hell I'll agree to something like that!"

"You have to, for the sake of appearances. You were smart not to try to help Myler."

"Don't flatter me," Crook warned.

"Just the same, it was the right thing to do," Sundance said. "The same goes for me if I get into trouble in New Mexico. If I ask you for help, answer back and tell me to go to hell. Where will you be?"

"Where will I be when?" Crook puffed on his cigar so furiously that his head was wreathed in smoke, a sure sign that he was angry.

"Where will you be, say in six weeks from now?"

"Denver," Crook said. "You've come up with some sort of plan, haven't you? Would it be too much to ask you what it is?" The chuck was begging for another biscuit, and Crook turned his wrath on the rodent. "Didn't I tell you to be gone, you furry little bugger?"

The chuck twittered, not at all frightened. Sundance said, "No plan as yet, Three Stars. All right, a plan of sorts. But only if it looks as if nothing else will work."

Crook hurled a biscuit at the chuck. "You refuse to tell me about this 'sort-of' plan of yours?"

"That's right, sir," Sundance said. "If I get into trouble you must disown me. You can't help me, and you won't."

"After all the years we've been friends, who's going to believe such a thing?"

Sundance said, "They'll believe it if I do something bad enough."

"You're not going to piss on the flag, are you?"

"No, I'd get lynched for that," Sundance said,

smiling at Crook's idea of the ultimate crime. He liked this crusty old soldier very much. Men like George Crook should be the leaders of nations. But they weren't, more's the pity. The man had lived an honorable, useful life. He fought the Indians hard when he had to; always his victories were tempered with mercy. To get him involved in a jail-breaking conspiracy would be a disaster. If the story ever came out, his career in the army would be finished. The vultures of the Indian Ring, ever waiting for a chance to destroy him, would tear him to bits with their dirty talons.

"What is this terrible thing you're going to do?" Crook persisted.

"I haven't worked it out yet."

"God Almighty!" Crook roared. "Never have I met a man so stubborn. You wouldn't be related to Stonewall Jackson, by any chance?"

"I thought *you* were," Sundance said. "Three Stars, I won't let you get mixed up in this. I must have your word that you won't try to interfere."

"Go to blazes," Crook growled.

"I won't start without it, Three Stars," Sundance said quietly. "You'll mess me up if you try to help. It has to be done alone."

"All right then," Crook said, after thinking about it. "You have my word. I guess you know what you're doing. You usually do."

Sundance got up from the table. "Next time I'll fry the fish, Three Stars. You may be a great general but you're a rotten cook."

Crook glared at him. "You mean you're leaving right now? You just got here, you madman."

"It's a long way to New Mexico," Sundance said.

Chapter Two

THE prison stood high on a hill above the Rio Grande. It was early in the morning, and Sundance watched it through field glasses from a long way off. Squat, ugly, seemingly impregnable, the jail dominated the tiny town of Sanderson like the fortress it was. It was bigger than he expected it to be, and the walls enclosed a stunted cliff far to the rear. The walls, at least twenty feet high, looked thick enough to withstand artillery; it seemed to be a part of the rock it was built on. The hill was bare of anything that might provide cover to escaping prisoners, and even the cemetery at the bottom contained no grave markers.

On all corners of the walls were guard towers manned by riflemen and Gatling gunners. For continuous fire it took two men to operate a Gatling gun: one to load, one to turn the firing crank. If they knew their business, and he guessed they did, they could lay down an incredible rate of fire, sweeping the approaches to the prison in every direction. The river made its way between the prison and the town on the other bank. There were two bridges, the town-built bridge as well as the Santa Fe Railroad bridge. In this part of New Mexico the river was shallow, as it was for most of its length; it could be waded without any difficulty by a man who wasn't being chased by a hail of bullets from rapid-fire guns. The town of Sanderson was on a spurline of the Santa Fe, and trains were infrequent. Sundance had a printed train schedule, and after watching the bridge for two days, he knew it was accurate. The depot was in the town, but few passengers got on or off the trains that passed through.

He had taken great pains not to be spotted during his surveillance of the prison. He wanted to get a closer look at the town, but that wasn't possible. A white man, even an Indian, might be able to affect some sort of disguise; Sundance knew it would not work for him. With his dark skin, the color of an old penny, his great height, his pale blue eyes and shoulder-length yellow hair, there was no chance of going unobserved. Once seen, he would be fixed in people's minds.

The town lived off the prison. The prison was its only reason for being, for prisoners had to be fed, however badly, and there would be other prison-related businesses: lumber, adobe brick, harness, clothing, the various articles manufactured in the blacksmith shop and the mattress works. He had a pamphlet on the prison; in its way, the Cage was famous. Celebrated badmen had been hanged there, for it had an execution-shed, and condemned men were brought from all over the territory to have their necks stretched by the scientific method perfected by Berry in England. No longer did men strangle at the end of the rope, said the pamphlet. Before they were hanged they were weighed, the thickness of their necks taken into consideration; and when the trapdoor was dropped they went to heaven or hell, depending on their preparations for the hereafter, with the ease of someone falling off a log.

Sundance knew the pamphlet by heart, having read it

so many times. It had been published five years before, and so it wasn't as reliable as it might have been. Still, it was reliable enough for his purpose, which was to learn everything he could about Sanderson Penitentiary, never referred to (in the pamphlet) as the Cage, the name by which it was best known. There was a section for women, mostly murderers and bandits, but it was much smaller than the quarters provided for the men. Most famous among the women prisoners was the Mexican lady highwaywoman Maria Campo who had cut out her philandering husband's heart and slapped him in the face with it after the deed was done.

Sundance moved the field glasses from one guard tower to another. At night, as soon as it got dark, naphtha lights flared inside and outside the walls. The white lights were reflected in the river and they washed the bridges and the town with their merciless glare. Even the black, oily smoke from the trains were no match for the lights. The prison had only one gate, but there was another gate behind it. There was a sally port in the main gate, and when prisoners were passed through they were forced to strip between the gates. Lawmen who brought prisoners were not allowed to pass through the second gate; there was a barred window for commitment papers to be passed through, signed and returned. Both gates were made of steel, criss-crossed and immensely heavy. Watching for two days, Sundance saw prisoners young and old, some women, going in guarded by U.S. marshals or town marshals. It was easy to tell the federal lawmen from the village policemen—the federal men always looked tougher, and moved in a different way.

Sundance saw a Mexican Indian who seemed to have the run of the place. He wasn't uniformed like the guards in the towers or in the tower that stood outside the walls. This tower was higher than the others, and it was manned by riflemen who moved on open cat-walks night and day. Like the other towers, there was a Gatling gun on a swivel.

So this Mexican Indian isn't a guard, Sundance thought. He wasn't sure that he hadn't seen him before. On the second day Sundance watched the prison, the Mexican came out with three dogs and took them down the hill and over the bridge and away from the town. A tracker. That was it. The Mexican was a tall man, anyway, tall for a Mexican, and he wore an ordinary range hat and cowhand's clothes. When he took out the dogs he carried a whip, but he didn't use it, and he stood patiently while one dog took a long time to squat. Sundance knew he had seen the Mexican a long time before, but he couldn't put a name to the face.

At no time were both gates open, and whenever a wagon came or went, the riflemen who walked the platform behind the walls came forward to train their carbines on people going in or out. The Gatling gun in the outside guard tower turned, too, ready to fire if something started up.

That's why the tower is there, Sundance thought. The Gatlings in the other towers can't cover the gate. If a prisoner makes it through the gate, the Gatling in the outside tower will cut him down.

There would be a steam-whistle, he knew. There was a steam engine in the jail; the alarm whistle would be hooked up to that, and once the whistle blew, the town of Sanderson would come alive. Sanderson would be a bounty town, as what prison town was not? Not everyone would turn out to hunt an escaped prisoner, but most would. Sundance knew other prisons, and they always had a deal with the towns that lived off them. Bring them back any way you can: dead or alive. Preferably dead, because there was nothing like a rotting man on the back of a mule to put the fear of God into other prisoners with escape on their minds.

The prison was in Dona Ana County, about one hundred miles north of the Mexican border; a man could follow the river to El Paso. But they would be watching the river because it was the easiest way to go. The railroad ran down to El Paso, and from there all the way to Mexico City. The railroad was just as dangerous, Sundance thought. They would search the trains going south; the telegraph lines would be used to speed descriptions to all parts of the territory.

Head east into the desert, Sundance thought. That was the route to take. But he didn't like the look of the Mexican tracker. Men like that were single-minded, cruel, relentless, and always took great pride in what they did. Sundance didn't want to kill the man, yet it might come to that if he pressed them too hard.

In his two days of scouting the prison, Sundance formulated and discarded many plans for getting Myler out. It just couldn't be done from the outside. Blaisdell, the superintendent, seldom left the jail, so he couldn't be kidnapped and traded for Myler. Besides, Blaisdell might refuse to trade even with a gun at his head, and if this plan failed, there would be no chance of trying another. Myler would be locked up so securely that he would never again see the light of day.

It would have to be worked from the inside. This was something he seemed to have known all along, much as he dreaded the idea. Sundance had been in other jails, mostly in the wild, drunken days of his youth before Crook bullied him away from the bottle; had in fact threatened to have him shot if ever he got drunk again. He smiled when he recalled Crook's furious warnings.

To be sent to the Cage, he would have to commit a serious crime. Drinking and fighting would not be enough. All that would have to be worked out. The thought of going to prison made him shudder, and it wasn't the brutality and the bad food, the stink of the slop buckets, the howling of the insane. All that was bearable. More than anything, he feared being penned up; the crashing of cell doors, the turning of keys in locks, sounded in his head. All his life he had roamed the West a free man, doing what he wanted to do, always moving on when his work was done. He hated towns, and what was a prison but a town with all the faults of town life magnified ten thousand times? Yet he had to go to jail; there was no other way he could think of. The jail could be taken, but it would take many men to do it. He knew men he could hire—the border towns were full of hard cases willing to do anything for a price —but that would mean killing, for there was no way to silence the Gatling guns in the towers.

He realized that he had no plan of escape from the inside. The routine of the place would have to be studied. That would take time: days, weeks, maybe months of planning.

He was a halfbreed and would be treated like one, and not just by the guards but by the prisoners. He would be recognized by someone as soon as he passed through the gates. He was too well known to remain just another convict. The hard cases would gang up on him, and if he didn't fight back it could only get worse. There would be fights and he would lose some of them. Still, it had to be done.

A train crossed the bridge and freight was unloaded at

the depot. After that, it was quiet again. Not much later, the main gate of the prison opened and a trusty, an old man, came out pushing a handcart and escorted by a shotgun-toting guard. There was a body in the cart, and as the cart was going down the hill to the cemetery, a burly man in black crossed the town bridge and waited with a Bible in his hand.

The trusty tilted the cart and the body tumbled into a grave already dug, and after the dirt was shoveled in, the minister read from the Good Book while the guard yawned. Then the trusty and the guard went back to the prison and the preacher walked over the bridge and back into town.

Sundance put the field glasses back in their case and went down the hill to where Eagle was waiting. It was hot and he gave the stallion water, and drank some himself. It was time—past time—to get on with it, but even while he rode away from Sanderson he hoped to think of some plan that would make it possible to free Myler without having to go to prison himself.

He rode east from the river, heading for a settlement about fifty miles away. What he had to do was to buy supplies and hide them along the escape route. Canned goods, guns and ammunition, blankets for the freezing nights on the desert. Canteens for water—above all, water. Horses? He hadn't figured that out yet. What kind of shape was Myler in? He didn't know. Myler had been in the Cage for nearly two months, and Crook said he wasn't a well man.

There were so many things he didn't know about Selden Myler. A narrow-chested man with carroty hair and an irritable manner, Myler wasn't easy to know, and was hard to like. Like so many men who were convinced of the rightness of their cause, he became furious if his judgments were questioned. Sundance knew he was from Michigan and was not friendly with his family, and that was all. He looked and sounded like a cranky lay preacher. He was capable of smiling, but always with a bitter twisting of the mouth that was more like a grimace. During his time at the reservation he was forever writing angry letters to the Eastern newspapers; it was a wonder that the Indian Ring hadn't gone after him before. Now this unlikable man was in the hottest part of hell.

The next day, Sundance rode into the town of Lemberg and bought nearly everything he needed for the escape. His list of supplies was a long one, and the storekeeper called off each item as he placed it on the counter.

"You sure must like beans," he said.

Down the street, Sundance bought three long-barreled Colts, .44 caliber, single action, and ammunition to go with them. There was always a chance that one of his caches of weapons and food would be rooted up by some animal or discovered by a prowling desert rat. So he bought three of everything. He bought whiskey in flat pint bottles, and although he hated liquor and its effect on him, he knew there were times when it was useful. Last of all, he bought a pack horse at the livery stable, a docile animal that wouldn't give any trouble.

Then he backtracked the way he had come, burying weapons and supplies. That done, he rode east again, mapping the escape route. He skirted the Mescalero reservation and headed straight into the desert. Once he was in the desert, away from the towns, he saw no one. This was brutal country, but he was well equipped and he crossed it without incident. The next time I come through here won't be so easy, he thought. If I get this far, I'll be lucky.

So many things could go wrong. You could work out what looked like a very good plan, and then from out of nowhere came something you never expected. Anything could do it. A man who couldn't sleep might be up and around in the dead of night; a dog might bark. You could take a hard fall and break a leg, and all your plans went out the window. Even so, he had to go through with it: he owed it to Myler.

Unless they were able to steal horses, the first part of the journey would have to be on foot. The guns and supplies could be left as long as it took to get out; horses were another story. Money was going to be an important part of the escape. Money and clothes.

They would head south once they crossed the desert, and they might have to go all the way east to the Pecos River before they could do that. He felt sure the local agents of the Indian Ring would hear about the escape the same day it happened. There would be the usual reward, posted by the territorial authorities, and the Indian Ring would sweeten the pot with a lot more. By himself, Myler wasn't such an important threat to the Ring, yet they would pursue him with the ferocity of their kind.

We may not make it at all, Sundance thought: the Gatlings may cut us down in the first minutes of the escape. As a jail, the Cage was the best of its kind, and the men who planned it, and the men who refined those plans, had left nothing to chance. It had the simplicity of a bullet in the brain.

Days later, on the other side of the desert, Sundance rode in to the town of Cíbola, a place more Mexican than American; a straggle of houses that didn't quite make up a main street. It was in the middle of nowhere, and it looked it. It had no bank, no marshal's office, and the old and crumbling Spanish church was the biggest building in town. Brown-skinned Mexican children were tying a can to a dog's tail when Sundance rode in. The dog ran away, howling, and the children pelted it with rocks.

Sundance looked for Dobson Getty and found him in the saloon he owned, years older now and looking as if he drank as much liquor as he sold across the bar. But for all his dissolute appearance, Getty was a miser, a man obsessed by money, and he had spent most of his life stealing it, saving it, and otherwise accumulating what he called a cushion for his old age. He had salted mines, married and swindled rich widows without benefit of divorce from his earlier victims. Accused of many crimes, among them gun-running, rustling, smuggling and fraud, he had spent very little time in jail, relying on his heartfelt belief that everyone was at heart a thief and could be bought for the right amount of money. Bribery was the best defense against any charge of wrong-doing, Getty always said; in his opinion, there was no such critter as an honest man. And Sundance knew him to be completely reliable once the money changed hands. He was a villain with a powerful sense of honor.

When Sundance went in to Getty's saloon, he heard him telling a Mexican sheepherder that if he bought his whiskey on credit he must expect to be charged more for what he drank. Getty was one of those men of no age: he might have been forty or sixty. In fact he was seventy-five, with an unlined brown face and a head of fine white hair that he dyed black or red or brown, according to his whim. At the moment it was red.

"Well, look who's here," he exclaimed when Sundance came in. "I was just explaining certain facts of finance to my friend Ramon. When you borrow money or goods you have to pay interest. Borrowing means bookkeeping, and that uses up a man's valuable time. Time is money, am I right?"

Sundance laid a silver dollar on the bar. "A bottle of beer for me," he said.

"It won't be cold," Getty said. "It'll be wet but it won't be cold."

The sheepherder went out in a rage and Getty said, "If I live to be a hundred I'll never understand Mexicans. Wine, women and song is a great idea, only they don't want to pay for it. How are things, Sundance? Been making any money?"

"Here and there," Sundance said. "I came to ask if you might be interested in something I have in mind. Have a drink, Dob."

"Well, I am glad to see you," Dobson Getty said, taking his special bottle from under the bar. "I hope what you have in mind isn't legal. What's legal don't usually pay so much. But I have to tell you that in my old age I have to be careful what I do, and that costs more."

Sundance sipped the warm beer. "You'll be paid what we agree to, Dob."

"That's the kind of talk I like to hear," Getty said. "A man gives his word, he'd be a fool to go back on it. How is that beer?"

"It tastes like you made it yourself."

"I did. I'm so far off the beaten track I have to make everything myself. I don't think it tastes too bad for a homemade brew. I take more care with the whiskey. I take care not to get caught by the revenue marshals. But there's not much chance of that. They hate to make the trip just to catch a harmless old fella like me. But it's agin the law, so I always have my Mexican friends scouting the country on all sides."

Sundance pushed the beer away and told Getty to get him a glass of water. "Been a few years since the last time we met. How do you stand with the law?"

"All right," Getty answered. "Haven't been in trouble lately, not for a dog's age. Anyhow, I never did anything that bad. The few times I got caught I did my time without bitching about it. Small potatoes. The longest I ever got was a year."

"You ever been in the Cage?"

"Good Lord! That place. Of course I haven't. I did my year in Fairfax. I'm telling you I never was important, as you ought to know by now. What's this about the Cage?"

There was no one else in the saloon. "I want to break a man out of there," Sundance said quietly.

"What did he do?"

"He was convicted or murder and got life. You don't have to know his name."

Getty poured a drink and downed it. "It's best I don't. Count me out if you're looking for help with the actual jail-break. I'd as soon get shot as land in the Cage, though I don't intend neither thing to happen. You're a good man, Sundance, but I don't think you can do it. Is it money or friendship that makes you talk so foolish?"

"He's a friend," Sundance said.

Getty scratched his head with his middle finger. "No man is that good a friend."

"You wouldn't be in on the break," Sundance said.

"You'd have nothing to do with it. I can pay a thousand dollars plus your expenses."

"My expenses will be considerable," Getty said. "I'll have to neglect my various businesses—money lost all over the place—if I have to travel a distance. What do I have to do?"

"You have to hold still for getting shot," Sundance said. "A nick in the arm."

Getty took another drink. "I think you better explain this," he said. "For getting shot, I ought to be paid a little more."

Chapter Three

GETTY said, "If I didn't know you better I'd think you were crazy. You *are* crazy. You want to go to jail for attempting to murder a man—me. You start in like the wild Indian you used to be and accuse me of swindling you in a horse deal. What horse deal? That part will have to be explained in court."

"I'm going to sell you my horse for next to nothing because I need the money to stay drunk. You'll get a bill of sale so it looks legal. You'll keep my horse here till I break jail."

The old man grinned. "What happens if you don't?"

"You get to keep the horse," Sundance said.

"I could make a lot of money with that stallion if I put him out to stud. That's not to say I hope you get killed. It's just that . . ."

"That's all right, Dob. I know you'll take good care of my animal no matter what happens."

"That I will. Tell me where this playacting is supposed to take place."

"Town of Clovis," Sundance said. "That way you won't be too far from home. You ever go there?"

"Now and then," Getty said. "I do a little business with certain parties that run stock over the Texas line. It's legal trading. I don't want trouble with the Rangers.

They have no jurisdiction here, but the Rangers have been known to cross borders with their badges in their pocket."

Sundance said, "Then you have a reason for being in Clovis. You go there two days before I come looking for you. Where will I find you?"

"In the bar of the Clovis Hotel. That's where I do most of my business after looking over the Texas stock. Mostly I'm there at night. You won't be too drunk, will you?"

"I'll look as if I've been drinking a lot," Sundance said. "But I won't be drunk when I nick you in the arm. Which arm, Dob?"

Getty rubbed his left arm. "This one," he said. "Just you make sure you don't have shaky hands. You going to fire more than one shot?"

"All six," Sundance said. "The last one will nick you. I'll keep trying to fire the empty pistol and you rap me on the head. A good rap, but don't crack my skull. Then the marshal shows up and I go to jail."

"You're lucky you picked Clovis," Getty said. "It has good law and you won't get lynched. You're a halfbreed, my friend. The judge will hit you harder than I will. The judge won't see you as just another drunken Indian. They like their Indians tame, and you were never that."

"I know what to expect," Sundance said, dreading the ordeal but ready to see it through.

"I hate to say this," Getty said. "But you might be better off creasing some upright citizen. My reputation is not as pure as the driven snow."

Sundance smiled at the ancient villain. "Your reputation will explain why I accuse you of cheating me. But you'll have the bill of sale, and that puts you in the clear. As soon as the trial is over, you come back here. Except for looking after my horse, your part will be finished."

Getty poured another drink but left it on the bar. "You won't take offense at what I'm going to ask you?"

"Ask away, Dob."

"All right then. You've never done much jail time, and what you did wasn't in the Cage. It's bad as bad can be. If it gets too bad and you can't get out, you could say the whole thing was rigged. No real horse deal, no real shooting. The the law would be coming for me. I'm too old to go back behind the walls." Getty drank his whiskey and wiped his mouth. "That's the question I'm worried about."

Sundance shook his head. "No need to dwell on it," he said. "I won't get your tail in a crack. But now that questions are being asked, let me ask one. That's a good horse, my horse. I wouldn't want you to get tempted and tell the wrong people the real reason why I'm in jail. If you did that, they'd hang chains on me and put me in a solitary cell. Just thinking out loud, Dob."

Suddenly they laughed. Getty said, after he wiped his eyes, "You'd break out for sure if I informed on you. I'm looking forward to a soft old age and I don't want to keep looking over my shoulder till they put me six foot under."

"I'll drink to that," Sundance said, and when the old man looked surprised, he added, "I have to start sometime to make it look real."

Getty smiled his crafty smile. "I'd like to get my money in advance," he said. "A thousand for getting shot, five hundred for expenses. Drinks are on the house. Just don't break up my place when you get to feeling wild. I'd have to charge you extra for that."

Riding the poorest animal in Getty's stable of horses, Sundance drank his way through all the towns between Cibola and Clovis. He ate nothing but a few handfuls of jerked meat, and within a week his face was haggard and his bones stuck out. His eyes were red-rimmed and he smelled, and in one town he was run out by deputies with sawed-off shotguns. The only weapon he carried was a long-barreled Colt .44; his other weapons—the thick bladed Bowie knife, straight-handled throwing hatchet and Winchester—were buried with the cache closest to the prison.

He hated the cheap whiskey he drank; it brought back so many bitter memories of the time when, drunk and crazed with grief, he had pursued the renegades who had murdered his parents. His father had been tortured, his mother raped and strangled. It had taken months to catch up with the killers. But he found them, and they died in all the agony he could inflict. There were no quick bullets; he used the knife. And when the killing was over, he roamed the country like a madman, drunk and dangerous, searching for his death, but he always came out alive because he was faster with a gun, deadlier with a knife than even the worst men he fought. Then Crook had locked him in a guardhouse and let him howl and vomit and crawl until the whiskey was out of his system. And when all that was over, and he was no longer wild, just sick and shaky, four of Crook's troopers put him under a pump and scrubbed him clean. That night he ate with Crook in his quarters.

It was the start of the long journey back.

The drinking frightened him more than any man that sought to take his life. For him, violent death was a constant companion, and he hardly gave it a thought except in the most practical way. But whiskey was a greater threat than bullets. He knew he couldn't handle it; this time he had to try. At night it gave him bad dreams from which he awoke in a lather of sweat. Usually he would be unable to get back to sleep once the nightmares came. Or if he did sleep, it was fitful and ghost-haunted, more exhausting than no sleep at all. There was a pink of whiskey in his saddlebag, but much as he craved it, he left it where it was. Only by day did he drink and always in some town or trading post where he would be seen. There was no use trying to fake his downfall, his disgrace; they had to believe what they saw—a dirty saddle-tramp with a thirst.

Two days from Clovis, he stopped drinking. By then his appetite was gone, but he forced himself to eat a trail stew made of jerked meat and raisins; solid food would have been impossible to hold down. That night he sweated clear through his blankets, then shivered as his temperature dropped. Toward morning he slept for a few hours and woke with a nerve-twanging headache and a terrible craving for something cold to drink. The water in his canteens was stale-tasting but he drank it greedily, wanting whiskey—just one small drink to set him up for the day. He didn't take it.

All day he sweated in the sun. He hated the way he smelled, but that was all to the good. That night he rode till hours past midnight, and by the time he rolled himself in his blankets he was exhausted. He slept well enough and would have slept more if the sun hadn't been shining in his eyes. The tremor had gone from his hands and after he ate a small batch of trail stew he knew he was going to be all right.

The sun was going down when he saw Clovis in the

distance. Gritting his teeth, he drank some whiskey to make his breath worse than it was. Then he put the bottle in his back pocket, making sure the neck stuck out for show.

Stone sober, he rode into town, swaying in the saddle.

He woke up in a cell. The sheriff was staring at him through the bars. "You stinking halfbreed," the sheriff growled. "Why'd you have to come to my town and start trouble?"

Sundance passed his tongue over his lips. "I want a drink of water." His voice sounded cracked. "For Christ's sake, give me some water."

The sheriff was a short, solid man with a bedraggled mustache. "I'm surprised you don't call for whiskey. You smell like you've been soaking in the stuff. You know what you did?"

"Got into a fight," Sundance said. "To pay the fine you can sell my horse. Give me some water and let me out of here."

The sheriff's eyes narrowed. "You did more than start a fight, halfbreed. You tried to kill a man. It's a wonder you didn't succeed. You fired six times and hit him once in the arm. You can thank the whiskey for your bad aim. We'd be hanging you if not for that. Nobody cares if you remember or not. You did it, all right. No end of witnesses."

Sundance rubbed his eyes and stared back at the sheriff. "Dobson Getty. I remember. Sheriff, that old man cheated me!"

"You kept saying that, it seems. I don't care who was cheated and who wasn't. Getty showed me a bill of sale that looked legal enough. Your name is Sundance. Jim Sundance?"

"I'm Sundance. Getty gave me a raw deal. I was drunk and he took advantage of that."

The sheriff got a dipper of water and passed it through the bars. Two shotgun deputies came and stood close. "You should have taken Getty to court," the sheriff said. "And not come here to make trouble."

One of the deputies laughed before the sheriff silenced him with a frown. "Let the judge decide," the sheriff said. "Attempted murder is the charge. Destruction of property is another. Paying for what you destroyed is the least of your worries. You had five dollars on you when we took you in. That won't take you far, not that you're going anyplace. Now drink the water so I can get you in front of the judge. Want some free advice? Don't ask for a jury trial. It costs money and the judge doesn't like to waste time."

"Will I get a fair shake from the judge?"

"A fairer shake than if you ask for a jury."

Sundance nodded, drinking the last of the water. "I'll do what you say, Sheriff. About that five dollars. Will you send a telegram for me?"

"Maybe," the sheriff said cautiously. "Depends what you say in it. Who's the party you want to get it?"

The sheriff's eyes widened when Sundance told him. "You must be crazy. What would the general want to do with the likes of you?"

The deputy who had been laughing started up again. Sundance said, "I served as chief scout for General Crook. He'll help me if he can. Tell him the fix I'm in, what the charge is, how this trouble got started. Tell him to telegraph the judge and explain that I'm all right."

"You sure want a lot for five dollars," the sheriff said irritably. "Don't be telling me how to send a telegram. I've sent more than you have. Where is Crook?"

"Army headquarters, Denver, Colorado. I'd be obliged if you got it on the wires before the judge hits me with a long sentence."

The sheriff reached for the empty dipper. "You're going to get a stiff sentence no matter what the general says. Put the handcuffs on him, boys. Shoot him dead if he tries to make a break."

They walked him across the town square to the courthouse, a brick building that looked new. On the patchy lawn stood the usual Civil War cannon and stack of rusting balls. Courthouse loungers stared at him as he passed with his heavily armed escort. Spring had edged into summer and it was hot.

The wounding of Dobson Getty was the most excitement the town had seen in a long time; all the benches in the courtroom were filled and men were standing in the back. Sundance's case had been moved up to the head of the docket as befitting a man charged with a serious crime. At 8:55 the judge, a portly man, bustled in and took his place on the bench. The bailiff declared the court to be in session and proceeded to read the charge.

The judge stared down from his perch. "You do not have a lawyer?"

Sundance was nudged to his feet by the sheriff. "No, your honor," he answered.

That seemed to please the judge. "Do you realize the seriousness of the charge?"

"Yes, your honor."

"Then how do you plead?"

"Can I put that off?" Sundance asked, getting a laugh from the spectators. The judge used his gavel until there was silence. "I'd like to hear what the witnesses have to say, your honor."

The judge was less pleased now. "You have the right

to be tried in front of a jury."

"No jury, your honor," Sundance said. "I'll take my chances with the court."

"So noted," the judge told the clerk. "Is the prosecution ready?"

A small waspish man stood up at the prosecutor's table and said he was ready. "My first witness is the wounded man, Dobson Getty."

Getty, his left arm bandaged, took the witness stand and was sworn in. Now and then he gave Sundance a look of great indignation. The prosecutor led him through his paces. Getty, seeming angry, denied that he had cheated the accused in the horse deal. "He came to me without hardly a cent in his pocket and said he wanted to sell his horse. An animal that was less valuable was to be a part of the deal. His own horse had been hard used but could be fed back to good health. I know horses, so I knew that. I offered him a hundred dollars and a fair-to-middling horse. Nobody asked him to come to me. That was my deal and he took it."

"Do you have the bill of sale?"

"Sure I have it." Getty took the bill of sale from his pocket and handed it to the prosecutor. "That's his signature right there."

Getty went on to say that he was having a drink in the bar of the Clovis Hotel when the accused came in "shouting drunk" and demanded the return of his horse.

"I told him a deal was a deal," Getty continued. "I bought the horse fair and square and nobody was going to take it away from me. I warned him I'd have the law on him if he didn't stop bothering me."

"Then what happened, Mr. Getty?"

"I got shot, sir."

"Yet you managed to subdue the accused in spite of your wound."

"I belted him across the skull. What was I supposed to do? Stand there till he reloaded his pistol?"

That brought more laughter, and Getty was excused. Other witnesses were called: a bartender and two men who had been drinking with Getty. They all agreed that Sundance was "crazy drunk" when he entered the bar. Six shots were fired, five shattering mirrors and bottles; Getty was wounded by the sixth.

"All the time Sundance was shooting he kept yelling, 'You've cheated your last man,'" the bartender testified, and the two other witnesses backed his statement.

The judge leaned forward in his high-backed chair. "Enough," he said. "This court has heard all the testimony it needs to hear. The accused will stand."

"How do you plead?" the judge asked.

"Guilty, your honor," Sundance answered.

"As well you might," the judge said. "This court would have found you guilty in any event. You stand here convicted of the most serious crime in the statutes, short of murder itself. Not only was your action without justification, the victim of your murderous assault was a man of advanced years. Obviously you are a man of lawless and dangerous disposition. The year is 1885, but you do not seem to be aware of it. There is no place for you in a society of laws. Therefore, it is my duty to see that you are removed from it. I hereby sentence you to seven years in the territorial penitentiary at Sanderson. Bailiff, call the next case."

On the way back to the jail the sheriff said, "You didn't do too bad. He might have sent you up or ten, even fifteen. Pleading guilty saved you a lot of time."

"Will you send the telegraph message to Crook?"

"I'll send it," the sheriff said. "Soon as I get you locked up, I'll send it. What harm can it do? A man facing what you are deserves that much, I guess."

"When do we start for Sanderson?"

"First thing in the morning. No more questions, I'm telling you. It's a long, rotten trip and you're the cause of it. But I'll send the God-damned message. If he's where you say he is, there should be an answer by morning."

Sitting in his cell with a tin plate of beans, Sundance thought, Well, that part of it is over. He guessed the sheriff would send the message to Crook, if only out of curiosity. Just sending the message would make the sheriff feel important. The sheriff was lazy but decent enough in his gruff way.

It was getting dark and down the corridor a drunk was babbling in his cell. There was a smell of creosote in the jail; the only light came from two hanging, tin-shaded lamps in the hall. Sundance finished the beans and stretched out on the thin mattress. For an instant there was a rush of panic and the walls seemed to close in on him. It passed quickly and, erasing all thought from his mind by an effort of will, he fell into a deep sleep.

Late that night he awoke when he sensed someone standing outside his cell. It was the sheriff and he had a yellow Western Union envelope in his hand. "I was making my rounds so I stopped by to give you this. I've read it so I know what it says. You can't have it because it goes with the papers I take to the jail."

Sundance lay with his hands behind his head. "What does it say, Sheriff?"

Without removing the message from the envelope, the sheriff said, "It's short. General Crook says, 'There is nothing I can do for you. I can't and I won't.'"

Sundance turned his face to the wall. "That miserable Bible-reading son of a bitch!"

Ten days later he was delivered to the Cage in handcuffs and leg-irons.

Chapter Four

BETWEEN the gates of the prison, Sundance was forced to strip, then told to spread his legs and lean against the wall so he could be probed for money or a sheathed knife. There were two guards; one held a sawed-off shotgun while the other did the work. They were powerful men of brutish appearance and not much intelligence. In their dark blue uniforms, with their heavy well-fed faces, they might have been brothers.

Running his fingers through Sundance's hair, the searcher said, "You're overdue for a haircut, halfbreed." He slammed a patched canvas prison suit at Sundance and told to put it on. A pair of cheap prison-made boots went with the clothes.

"Why don't you ask for socks?" the other guard said. "Some of the trash that come in here think they should get socks."

The inner gate wasn't unlocked until the sheriff left with his deputies. Sundance looked at the buildings he was marched past, trying to relate them to what he had read in the pamphlet. The main cellblocks were easy to identify. One story high and built of adobe brick, they had slatted steel doors but no windows. He identified the blacksmith shop by its sound: the furious clanging of metal. He looked up the hill toward the cliff and saw there were cells set into its face—caves or blasted-out holes with steel doors.

"Don't be looking up there, halfbreed," one of the guards said. "You'll land there soon enough. Pick up your feet, you red nigger! We don't have all day."

They unlocked a door and kicked him into a cell that was almost in darkness. After the door slammed and his eyes adjusted to the bad light, he was able to make out a man sitting on the edge of a bunk. The other bunks were empty.

"Welcome to the Cage," the convict said. "I am Kirby Goodhue Maitland, but everyone here calls me the Actor, an appropriate name since that is, or was, my profession. What would your name be, if I may ask?"

The man's voice was indeed actorish, full of stresses and dramatic pauses. Probably not a very good actor, Sundance thought. He didn't sound hostile. He might be a madman, and he might be a spy.

"My name is Jim Sundance," he said.

"An interesting name. Indian, I suppose. I don't mean to pry. It's simply that there isn't much to talk about in here. You are not a pervert, I hope. If you are, please accept my apology."

"Women were always enough for me," Sundance said.

"Too much for me," the Actor said. "Alas, I have not caressed a woman's body for fifteen years. There are women here, but they're hard to get at. Some you wouldn't want to get at. I see you're looking around your new home. Your eyes will get used to the light and you'll be able to see better. The cell you're in is nine feet by eight. It has a low domed ceiling. Why it's domed I have no idea. Perhaps because the building is made of adobe. Of course, it's no ordinary adobe. No straw is used in the bricks so it bakes as hard as rock. Ask me anything about the Cage. In here there are two tiers of bunks, three bunks to a tier. Steel. That foul-smelling thing against the wall—can you see it?—is the shit-bucket. It is emptied once a day and has to serve six men when we have a full roster. Soon it will be very hot and the bucket will stink worse than it does now. Then the big blueflies get in and drive you crazy with their buzzing and crawling. In the hottest part of the summer it can climb to 120 in the shade. Sometimes it's still over a hundred at midnight.

"You sweat until you think you can't sweat any more," the Actor went on, obviously enjoying himself. "But you keep on sweating, and if you don't get enough water, enough salt to keep a balance in the body, you die. Men the guards have a grudge against never get enough water, enough salt. It's murder, but nobody cares. In winter it's bitter cold. They take your pallet and blanket away from you in summer. When winter comes, you get them back. Scant comfort, I can assure you. The blankets are thin and worn, so you sleep with your boots on, or risk frostbite. Catch a cold and it turns to pneumonia. Pneumonia and consumption are the big killers here. The Indian prisoners have no immunity to consumption, and they die like flies, infecting everybody around them. We have men here who are being rotted to death by the pox. The wages of sin."

The Actor laughed crazily. "Official death is brought about by our whitewashed gallows room, very clean except when the condemned shits his pants. However, they don't do that any more. The odor displeased Mr. Blaisdell—he's our distinguished superintendent—and so he decreed that no candidate for the scaffold be given anything to eat for two days before his execution. So you might say that the grand old tradition of the condemned-man-ate-a-hearty-meal is without honor in this bower of bliss. But you mustn't think that Mr. Blaisdell is a totally black-hearted fellow. Condemned men are permitted the consolation of Reverend Zimmerman's company in their last moments. Indeed, Reverend Zimmerman is thrust upon them, be they Unitarian, Papist, Moslem, Buddhist or Chinee. We have no Moslems or Buddhists, but we do have one affluent Chinaman, a Santa Fe merchant who did his beloved to death with a hatchet. Reverend Zimmerman is of the Southern Baptist persuasion, a man of the cloth who firmly believes that our merry little planet came into being no earlier than three thousand years ago, all evidence, geological and otherwise, to the contrary. Reverend Zimmerman hates sin and loves money. He gets a fee for burials and Sunday services. His brother is in the territorial legislature. Need I say more?"

"Does money work here?" Sundance asked.

"Money works everywhere, my dear sir. From the hallowed halls of Congress to this sun-baked dungheap, money works. The eagle should not be the symbol of our glorious country but the dollar sign. You can buy just about anything here if money is provided by friends or business colleagues outside the walls. The rich Chinaman I spoke of never runs short of opium, thanks to the loyalty of his many sons. Others, mostly members of bandit gangs, train robbers and so forth, are looked after by their former associates. Not all, of course, but some. So there is honor among thieves. The captain of the guard, Tyson, controls the graft here with the help of his Quasimodo, the hump-backed McDuffie, who arranges how the money is to be paid. Liquor may be procured for a price. A very high price. So can potaguaya, otherwise known as marijuana, the Mexican weed so popular with our Latin prisoners. Women are available, but that costs more than anything else. By women I mean our women prisoners, for even Captain Tyson isn't bold enough to risk bringing prostitutes from beyond the gates. I have no friends with money, no friends of any kind, so all these years I have been celibate. Now I no longer have the urge. It passes, as do all things."

"But I always heard the superintendent was so straitlaced," Sundance said.

"Oh, he isn't in on the graft, if that's what you mean. At least, I don't think so. His principal concern is to run the prison as efficiently as he can. To him the thought of a prisoner escaping is as abhorrent as pork is to a devout Hebrew. In order to ensure the loyalty of his men, he allows them to graft to their hearts' content, provided they don't go too far. Everyone gets his share. Naturally the captain gets more than the others, but they all get enough."

"Why haven't the men with outside money, a lot of it, been able to buy an escape? It's been done in other prisons."

"It's been tried," the Actor said. "But no one ever got out that way. When Captain Tyson first arrived here, he gathered in a lot of money by arranging to let men escape by means of some scheme. The money was paid, yet in all cases the poor prisoner continued to languish in durance vile. So you see, our captain no longer is trusted by the criminal fraternity, not when it comes to escape plans. But he makes up for the loss of income in other ways. Indeed he does. I don't say he isn't tempted to let one or two men escape, but he is too frightened of the superintendent to give in to it. I've heard of a talk they had one time—some trusty overheard it, they say. Mr. Blaisdell warned the captain what would happen to him if any prisoner escaped, even if he wasn't in on the deal. The captain said that wasn't fair and Mr. Blaisdell said he didn't give a damn about fair. He said he had enough on the thieving captain to send him to prison for life. And where do convicts go when they get life? The Cage. That's enough to chill any man's blood, especially Tyson's; the men he flogged and tortured, most of them are still here. Not only that, the new captain might decide to kill him. So you see why there are no escapes."

"Who's the convict boss?" Sundance asked.

"The Cage is ruled by Wade Bracken and his thugs," the Actor said. "Old Wade is a sodomite of the most brutal kind. They say he was one before he came in here, not that he was jailed for corn-holding little boys. They say he likes them very young, babes in arms almost. However, there are no boys here younger than sixteen, so old Wade has to make do with what's available."

"What's he in for, Actor?"

"For killing four Mexicans for fun. This was not a major crime in the opinion of the court. All he got was ten years. It was murder—what else can it be called?—but old Wade's high-powered lawyer got it reduced to manslaughter. There was provocation, you see. They were Mexicans, after all, and that in itself is enough to offend the sensibilities of any real American."

Sundance decided the Actor wasn't a spy for anyone. But he sure was careless with his mouth. "How could they make manslaughter out of killing four men?"

"There were extenuating circumstances," the Actor said, and his shoulders shook with silent laughter. "Old

Wade got drunk and decided to put on a William Tell show. Bored, I suppose. Whatever the reason, old Wade rounded up four Mexicans in the town of Manzanilla—Mexicans are few there despite the name—and proceeded to shoot apples off their heads. A correction, sir. They were potatoes, not apples. The four trembling Mexicans were lined up against a wall, with most of the town watching, making bets and having a very good time, as Americans will. But it would seem that old Wade changed his mind at the last moment. He's an expert shot. He shot the four men through the head, neat holes in the forehead. Initially charged with murder, old Wade's lawyer pleaded human error. Poor old Wade had been drinking and his hand was not as steady as it should have been."

"I'm surprised he didn't get off," Sundance said. "In that part of the territory it shouldn't have been so hard."

"You're right, sir," the Actor said. "The judge, so I hear, wanted to turn him loose with a stern warning. I can see the jurist's point of view, as I'm sure you can. After all, anyone can make a mistake—and don't forget that old Wade is an old-fashioned land baron—but the governor, embarrassed by the whole unfortunate affair, let it be known that old Wade must be sent to prison in order to discourage others who might use Mexicans as targets. Some of the territorial legislators are of Spanish origin, pure Castillian, of course. So old Wade's sentence wasn't all the governor's idea."

"How much of the ten years has he served?" Sundance asked.

"A little more than two," the Actor said. "There is talk of a parole. Why not? Old Wade is one of the biggest ranchers in the territory, and the rights of such men must be respected, for after all, old Wade is no common criminal, no vulgar housebreaker, no furtive passer of base coin. Just the same, life here isn't too bad for old Wade. He has a cell to himself, a bed instead of a bunk, an oil lamp, a table and other furniture, a carpet on the floor. At the moment he shares it with his latest youth, a feeble-minded pervert with a poetic expression but who is unable to read or write. It's a very nice cell, as cells go, a honeymoon cottage with many brides. Oh, I should have mentioned that it has a chemical water closet rather than a crap-bucket. More to the point: old Wade doesn't have to work and he's never been flogged or subjected to even lesser punishment. Perish the thought. And he gets mail and newspapers and tobacco. He even has a little alcohol stove on which his lads cook tasty meals. Whiskey, of course."

"Then he can do as he pleases?"

"All but walk out of here. A few months ago, he beat one of his boy-brides to death. The poor fellow was buried and not a question asked, not a tear shed, although Reverend Zimmerman did a bang-up job at the graveside. It was the old, old story: the little wifey committed sodomite adultery with some young man he liked better. The day after the burial, old Wade put his grief aside and married again. Life must go on."

"Why do you keep calling him old Wade?"

"Because he *is* old," the Actor said. "Oldish. Wade is sixty. A very virile sixty. It's not true that men improve with age. They don't, they get worse. As they get older they see death waving come-and-join-me, but they don't want to wave back. Old Wade's gang aren't all natural perverts, but all are perverts of necessity. It's an elite society and not just any Greek-minded fellow is permitted to join. Even in prison there is the caste system."

Sundance said, "Besides Wade, who's the worst in the bunch?"

"A brute who calls himself Mingo," the Actor said. "It may even be his real name. An apprentice strongman in some traveling show, he might have made a great career if he hadn't broken the manager's spine while surprised in the act of looting the cash-box. He got life. Long divorced from old Wade, he remains a high-ranking member of the palace guard."

"He pimps for Wade?"

"Pimping is one of his jobs. In his way, he's like those fellows who loiter in the lobbies of tenth-rate hotels—the hotels where the out of work actresses live. Waitresses down on their luck. Country girls come to the big city to search for alcoholic fathers. Little matchgirls. Orphans of the storm."

"You lay it on pretty thick, Actor," Sundance said.

"No," the Actor said. "I don't. What I am is a cheerful pessimist. Watch out for Mingo. Truthfully, I can't say what you should do if he approaches you, and I'm sure he will. You are a good-looking man in a battered sort of way. It might be better if you gave in without a fight. Would you prefer to fight? What did you do to get in here? Often a man's crime determines his standing in the convict community."

"Attempted murder," Sundance said. "I got drunk and tried to kill a man who had cheated me. I got seven years."

The Actor laughed. "You should have done something much more desperate. Train robbers and murderers are the aristocrats of the Cage. You didn't even kill a man. If Mingo approaches you, it might be better to get it over with. He will tire of you after a while."

"You've been through it?"

"Oh yes," the Actor answered wearily. "When I first

came here fifteen years ago, I was not as I am now. Women liked me. They thought I looked like Edwin Booth. Old Wade wasn't here then, but there were other Wades. I was twenty-two, young-looking for my age, not unhandsome. I got buggered many times. My first encounter was with seven of them. One held a sharpened six-inch nail to my throat while the others took turns."

The Actor went on. "The only way I could get rid of the perverts was to age as quickly as I could. Conditions here made that easy. Also, I made myself dirtier and smellier than the rest of the prisoners. After that they let me alone, all but a few for whom filth acts as an aphrodisiac. But they were seldom young and strong, and so I was able to fight them off. Now I am a grand old man of thirty-seven. With age has come serenity. Do I smell as badly as I think I do?"

"I just smell that bucket," Sundance answered. "You asked me what I did. What did you do?"

"I committed the sin of patricide," the Actor answered. There was a touch of pride in his voice.

"You killed your father?"

"It happened because of my father's fourth wife, a comely creature a few years older than myself. I thought I couldn't live without her at the time, but her name escapes me now. Perhaps it was Dolores. Great thunderbolts of menace were hurled at me by Father and, fearing for my life—he was a violent man—I introduced ground glass into his stew. It went off smoothly and he was buried without fuss. If I hadn't asked Father's lady for a share of the inheritance, I would not be here now. Outraged by my modest request, she denounced me to the authorities and testified against me at my trial. The exhumed the body, found traces of glass—and Good night, Sweet Prince. The judge was especially severe; Americans loathe poisoners. He sentenced me to one thousand years. Judges can do that if they feel like it. This one did.

"I suppose I shouldn't have poisoned Father," the Actor said. "I had no formal education, none at all, not even the McGuffey Reader. But my peripatetic pater insisted that I memorize *all* of Shakespeare. At least the major plays. And I did, as I did those of many other playwrights. My father was a renowned chewer of scenery. He called himself 'an interpreter of the classics.' Interpreter, my foot! When he played Hamlet, he made the Melancholy Dane a man of action. No farting around for *his* Hamlet. No indedisiveness there. He discovered comedy in King Lear and received rotten tomatoes for his pains. What he did to Macbeth was a crime. But audiences came to love him, as I did. Without a doubt he was the world's worst actor, a joke in the profession. I forgive him because he crammed the classics down my throat. Even today I am inspired by Shakespeare's divine flatulence. I am waterlogged with words. I have housemaid's knee of the brain. What else do you want to know?"

"Everything you know about this prison," Sundance said.

"I fear you are headed for trouble, Mr. Sundance," the Actor said. "You are a well-spoken man and a good listener, yet I sense the violence in you. Do not be violent here, if you know what's good for you. If you break the rules—there are so many rules—you will be sent to the Snake Hole. It was blasted from solid rock and can be entered only by a narrow passage. Day or night, it remains in total darkness. No light comes from the ventilation shaft, which is curved to keep the light out. Bread and water, nothing else. No bunk: you sleep on the floor. No crap-bucket. The guards who gives you your rations are forbidden to speak to you. If you stay long enough, you go insane."

"What about the snakes?"

"Rattlers crawl in through the ventilation shaft or are tossed in by the guards. Scorpions get in too. A man in shackles has no chance to defend himself. Many men die. Next to the Snake Hole is the Crazy Hole. The names mean nothing; they are quite alike. I have been in both. I graduated from anger to lunacy. But I survived, and in time they had to let me out to make room for others. I have survived everything, Mr. Sundance. After fifteen years, even Mr. Blaisdell has given up on me. They can't hang me for nothing, so, having survived the worst, there is nothing more they can do to me. Officially, I am out of my mind. I don't think I am. Do you think I am?"

"A little," Sundance said gently.

"Thank you, sir," the Actor said. "They are convinced I am mad because I refuse to work. Men such as myself, locked up night and day, get down on their knees and beg to be allowed to work. Any kind of work, even the rockpile."

"I can understand that," Sundance said. "But what do you do with your days and nights?"

"I read the great plays that are in my head," the Actor said. "That pleases me better than making bricks or mattresses. When you came in I was applauding Portia in *The Merchant of Venice*, although I must say Shylock, as a villain, seems mild when compared to Captain Tyson. That man, sir, is one of the great villains of the world. When he finally arrives in hell, he will replace Satan as head devil in no time at all.

"I have other mental activities which keep me busy," the Actor said, chuckling with satisfaction. "I am the historian of this garden spot, but they won't allow me pen and paper to write it, so of necessity it must be an oral history. It was like that in ancient Ireland, sir. The bards sang the unwritten history of their people."

The Actor spoke with the ease of a practiced lecturer, and Sundance knew all this had been said before. Many times. He tried to steer the Actor away from the bards of Ireland by saying, "Things may change if they ever make New Mexico a state. You could get out."

"That is quite unlikely," the Actor said, but he was back on the track. "You might call this place America's Devil's Island. Back in the Seventies, they decided they needed an escape-proof prison to hold the increasing number of murderers and highwaymen. Of course, most of the murderers were hanged, but not all. As you see, I escaped the gallows myself. After a lot of windy debate, the territorial legislature approved an appropriation of $25,000. They built the walls first, naturally. Then the money ran out—a little graft here and there—and so the prisoners had to build the rest of their jail. I was one of the first jailbirds to arrive here, one of the founding fathers, so to speak. We built stone cells to house fifty prisoners, enough space, it was thought at the time. But it was far from adequate; as the territory grew, so did crime increase. So, under the benevolent gaze of the superintendent and his guards, we kept adding more buildings, more cages. The superintendent had been living in a shanty. That was not a fitting abode for such an important personage, so we built him a fine cottage. Then we built quarters for the guards, a kitchen, a boiler and engine room. Over the years we added a blacksmith shop and a small mattress factory."

Sundance glanced at the steel slats of his narrow bunk. Nothing crawled on it. Then he remembered that bedbugs didn't come out during the day.

"They sell the mattresses on the outside," the Actor said. "Anything of value is sold outside the walls. We must do our best to be self-supporting, you see. The idea is to restore to us our pride in honest toil. I went along with this theory until I got tired of working.

"We built a permanent gallows and erected a flogging post," the Actor explained. "You didn't see either as you came in the main gate. But you will. You may not stand on the gallows, but you will go to the flogging post. We've all gone there in our time."

Sundance looked at the slightly-built windbag. "What did you get flogged for?"

"I'm not sure," the Actor said. "I think the superintendent detected defiance in my manner. Anyway, the charge was insubordination, and I got a dozen lashes for it. Here, that is considered light punishment. Other men have been sentenced to fifty lashes, some to more than that. I've seen men flogged unconscious, then revived and flogged again. Some of them died while hanging in chains from the post. You'll see that too. We all get to see it. It's an object lesson, you understand. Whenever there's a flogging we're turned out to watch. The superintendent superintends the flogging. Tyson—that's the captain of the guard—does the actual work. He must like it, for I've never known him to give the job to anyone else. A fine figure of a man, is Captain Tyson. The floggings keep him in shape, and of course there is the mental satisfaction to be considered. I don't think he'd change jobs, even if they offered to make him governor."

"Then the prison is never inspected?" Sundance said.

The Actor laughed, shaking his head at the same time. "Bless your innocence," he said. "Of course it isn't. I'm sure the super has to send in reports from time to time. Red tape is the life's blood of government. These reports may even be read by some minor functionary. But no one ever questions the super's authority. Why should they? He has a perfect record from the bureaucrat's point of view. No prisoner gets out of here unless he's released—or buried. The super can't kill all the prisoners, much as he'd like to, so men do get to walk out. However, about the same number of men are buried. You must have seen our pleasant little cemetery when they brought you in."

"I saw it," Sundance said. "Why are so many men buried there? Don't some families claim the bodies?"

"Some try, not knowing the rules of the place. But that too is contrary to the rules. I'm sure it's illegal, but the kinfolk of convicts usually don't have the money for lawyers. Most don't give a damn. So when you die here from natural or unnatural causes, the super sees to it that you're buried in quicklime. No coffin, not even a blanket. Coffins and blankets cost money. So you see, our superintendent tries to punish men even in death."

"You make everything sound so cheerful," Sundance said.

"Reality," the Actor said. "It takes a prisoner a long time to accept the reality of life here. Some never do. Some are so reluctant to face reality that they go mad and are locked up with the other loonies. Or they are killed. Looking at you, so big and hard-muscled, I think to myself, Now here's a man with escape foremost in his mind. He thinks all he has to do is figure out a plan that hasn't been tried before and he's off and running. Not so. All the old plans have been tried, and new ones invented. Ingenious plans; plans to be admired. Tunnels. Disguises. One man feigned death after eating some Mexican plant that slowed his heartbeat to nothing. But there was a catch to it—they buried him too deep for him to work his way out. Another brainy jailbird made a balloon in the mattress factory. They must have known about it, and they let him go ahead with the project. Poor fellow, he was lifting off nicely when the Gatling guns opened fire and brought him down like a duck. Take my word for it, sir. It can't be done. Don't try it unless you have a powerful urge to commit suicide."

"You've never tried it?" Sundance asked.

"I've thought about it often enough," the Actor said. "One of my old book-minded friends used to say that no problem is without a solution. How wrong he was, as I discovered to my dismay. When I first came here fifteen years ago, all my waking moments—my dreams, too—were filled with thoughts of escape. I tried to relate escape to mathematics, to logic, to the game of chess. Somehow I would *think* my way out of here. All nonsense. The walls are five and a half feet thick at the base, thirty feet high and built on a solid rock foundation. The walls are patrolled night and day by riflemen; all the towers are equipped with Gatling guns. Yet I remained convinced that I was going to break out. This fanciful notion persisted for a year. And then, sir, I gave up. I learned to face reality. You would be wise to do the same."

Sundance started to say something, but the Actor shushed him. "No more talk, sir. I think they're coming to get you."

Chapter Five

THE same two guards put handcuffs on Sundance and marched him to the superintendent's office in a small stone building separated from the others. On the way, he got a look at the superintendent's cottage and parts of the jail he hadn't seen before. The cottage was a well-made building of adobe and wood; it was surrounded by a high, spike-topped iron fence and the gate was secured by two enormous padlocks, the best they made, Sundance guessed. But it was the arsenal that interested him more than anything else. There would be blasting powder there as well as rifles, shotguns, ammunition. Two very old convicts pushing a cart loaded with sun-baked bricks stared at him, then looked away.

One of the guards knocked on the door which was opened by a man in civilian clothes. "New prisoner," the guard said.

"Pass him through and wait here," the civilian ordered. "Are the handcuffs and leg-irons secure?"

"Secure, yes sir," the guard answered in a bored voice, a man responding to ritual questions.

The civilian opened the door of the inner office and Sundance saw the stout wooden chair bolted to the floor. Wide leather straps hung down to the floor. They put Sundance in the chair and strapped him in until he was unable to move. The guards went out and Sundance found himself facing the man who ran the most brutal prison in the Southwest—the man he had to outwit.

Blaisdell had one arm and a face the color of dust; the room was bare except for a desk, a chair, two pale oak filing cabinets and a framed sign on the wall. The sign read: NO GOOD DEED GOES UNPUNISHED.

"I live by what that sign says," Blaisdell said in accent that could be from anywhere. His voice was flat and unemotional, almost tired, but absolutely relentless. He wore a light suit of Panama weave, a white shirt with a soft collar, a black cravat loosely tied and fastened with a silver pin. His face was clean-shaven and thin; small grey eyes, a long pinched nose.

"Which means I don't do any good deeds," Blaisdell explained needlessly. "Don't expect the smallest kindness from me. Break my rules and I will break you. Is that clear?"

"Yes sir," Sundance said.

"You see how powerless you are," Blaisdell said. "That's how you will be from now on. You have no power, no rights, no citizenship. Or, I should say, you are a citizen of Sanderson Penitentiary. Let me explain why I'm taking the time to talk to you. I want you to know how I run this prison so you won't have any doubts, any wrong ideas. In some of the other prisons you might have some appeal from my decisions. Here, there are none. The legislature has given me a free hand. Its members do not interfere because I do the job I'm paid to do. Oppose me or my men and they will turn you into a babbling idiot like Maitland."

"Maitland, sir?"

"The Actor. You were put in with him so he could tell you what it's like here. I'm sure he didn't spare you anything. He rambles but everything he said is true. In that he serves a useful function, the only reason he exists. He saves me time."

"Yes sir," Sundance said.

"Answer only when I ask you a question," Blaisdell ordered. He placed his hand on a cardboard folder on his desk. "I have your file. Attempted murder, the rest doesn't matter. An attempted murder means a murder which hasn't succeeded. This makes you a murderer in my eyes." He opened the folder. "It says here you served under General Crook in several Indian campaigns. Is that true?"

"Yes, sir."

"When I learned that General Crook had replied to your telegraph I made enquiries about you. You were a drunkard and a dangerous one before the general offered you his help. He got you to give up drinking after he picked you up out of the gutter. Why did you go back to the bottle? After so many years—you're no youngster—why did you do it?"

"Do I have to answer that, sir?" Blaisdell was bitter and conceited, and maybe he was too sure of himself, always a weak spot in any man's character.

"You will answer any question I put to you," Blaisdell said without raising his voice. "If I call the guards, you will be glad to answer."

Sundance said, "If you have my file, then you know I fought for the Indians for years. I earned and spent tens of thousands of dollars and there was nothing to show for it. Nobody trusted me, white or Indian. In spite of all I did, nothing changed. The Indians ran away from the reservations and were killed off or brought back like cattle. The tribes still fight among themselves, killing and raiding. I got sick of it, sir. I gave up."

Blaisdell closed the folder. "You didn't just give up or General Crook wouldn't have disowned you. A kindly man and a foolish one. You didn't just give up, you turned wild, drunken and dangerous. You won't be dangerous here, that I can promise you. I take absolutely no chances. That's why you're shackled and strapped in that chair."

The superintendent tapped his empty sleeve which was rolled up and fastened with a silver pin. "I didn't get a medal for this," he said. "However, I received a mild reprimand because losing my arm was bad enough. I lost the arm because I was careless—and kind-hearted. I was attached to the Provost Marshal's department in Washington. My job was to round up deserters hiding in the city. Faced by the savage Southerners, many of our boys in blue ran away. I had the bad fortune to catch one deserter, a middle-aged man with a wife and children somewhere. He cried and said the war frightened him and so he removed himself from danger. I pitied him, for we can't all be heroes. I didn't know he was wanted for robbery and murder as well as desertion. He appeared harmless enough, so I acted without caution. That's how he came to take my revolver away from me and shoot me with it. They caught him a few days later and, as a favor to me, since I was leaving the army, my colonel arranged it so I could pull the lever that sent him plummeting to eternity. He was the only man I've hanged personally. Over the years, as superintendent of this prison, I've watched many men drop to their deaths."

Blaisdell paused to rub the stump of his missing arm. "After they invalided me out of the army, my colonel got me the job here. They were building a new territorial prison and they needed a man with a firm hand." He gave Sundance a bitter smile. "I have only one hand but it's like iron. I've been here for fifteen years and no man has ever escaped from my custody, not for long anyway. Two men did get out in my first year here, when I was still learning how to keep them locked up. The two men got a little distance from here. My Apaches brought them back. Now I have a Mexican tracker that's better than any Apache. Have you ever heard the name Esteban Zorrilla?"

"Yes sir, he is a famous tracker." Now that he had the name, the other things he knew about Zorrilla came back to him. He had seen the man in Sonora during Crook's campaign against Geronimo. Zorrilla had been with the Mexican cavalry that accompanied the Americans. He had a fearsome reputation.

"Don't try to escape from here," Blaisdell said. "Even if you were to hold a pistol to my head, it wouldn't do you any good. My men will open fire no matter who's being held. That includes me."

The superintendent turned his back and stared out the window when the guards came to take Sundance to Captain Tyson's office. It was located in two cells that had been knocked together. Barred windows were set into the adobe walls; the inside had been painted white. There was a desk and chairs and a wash-stand with a china basin and jug. The stone floor was scrubbed and sanded. The captain of the guard was a sawed-off, runty man and he sat behind his desk like a block of wood. His uniform coat hung over the back of his chair; his cap was on the desk. A polished rock served as a paperweight for the files on his desk. He had the thick, oily skin of the heavy drinker, the belly of a glutton.

"This is the new one," one of the guards announced before Tyson waved him away.

Tyson had a granite jaw and shoulders as wide as a door. "You think you're a badman, eh?" he said. He cleared his throat and spat into a polished cuspidor. "We'll do our best to cure you of that. What can you do besides shoot people?"

"Break horses," Sundance answered. "I'm good with my hands. I can dress and butcher meat."

Tyson picked his teeth with a split match. "Forget the meat and the horses. You won't get close to neither. You say you're good with your hands. You had no money when you came in. You got any hid?"

"No sir," Sundance said.

"Then it's the rockpile for you," the captain decided. "If you can think of where money can be found, maybe I could fix you up in the mattress works. Or something like that. Think hard while you're up on that rockpile. Word can be got to friends on the outside. Friends, or somebody you know something about that would like to keep it quiet. A man can have friends he don't even know about. You had your warning from the super and it's too hot to repeat it. But I'll be watching you, half-breed."

The guards removed the handcuffs and leg-irons and marched Sundance up to the rockpile at the base of the cliff. On the way they passed convicts making adobe bricks in wood frames. They slapped the clay into shape and patted it into the molds; when the clay hardened in the sun, the bricks would shrink and could be removed. A pile of new bricks stood beside the row of molds ready to be loaded onto hand-carts. The sun was fierce and the wet clay steamed.

Sundance saw the Snake Hole and the Crazy Hole described by the Actor. He wondered where Myler was. Then he saw him as they neared the rockpile, which was made up of sheets of rock blasted down from the side of the cliff. The superintendent hadn't asked him about Myler, Sundance thought. Did he know of the old connection between them? Maybe not. He hadn't seen Myler for twelve years. There had been no communication of any kind, so it was possible that the superintendent hadn't linked them together in his mind.

Two guards with shotguns watched the ten men breaking rocks. They had the bored look of prison guards everywhere; boredom made them vicious. Myler, thin and hollow-faced, was swinging his sledgehammer with slow, tired movements. Some of the rock-breakers looked up quickly; Myler didn't.

"Got a red coon for you, Joe," one of Sundance's guards drawled. "I hear he's a bad 'n, so take care."

"Over there," the rockpile guard roared in mindless anger. "There's the sledge, there's the rocks. Get on with it. No talking, no resting till you eat. No talking then. I see you talking, you don't get to eat next time. Break the rocks small like the rest are doing."

Myler was still swinging his sledge, looking neither right nor left. Sundance wondered if Myler would recognize him when time came to eat. There was a chance he wouldn't, but for all he knew the superintendent might be watching them from a distance. There had to be some way of warning Myler before he blurted something out.

Sundance's hair had been clipped to a stubble, the baggy prison shirt hid the scars on his body, he was twelve years older, so he might go unnoticed. He swung the sledge, but it was a lot harder than it would have been a month before. Liquor and poor food had taken their toll and he found himself sweating and weak. Some of the other men were in worse shape; Myler was in the worst shape of all. In the rockpile gang were two Indians, two Mexicans. The others were white men of various ages. The Indians worked with innate fatalism, while the Mexicans broke the rocks as though breaking an enemy's head. After a while the guard called Joe came up close and watched Sundance, though there was no need. Not knowing what to say, he thought about it for a while. Then he spat on one of the rocks Sundance was sledging.

"You ain't breaking them rocks small enough," he drawled. "The rocks you're breaking is more special than the rest of them—they got to be smaller."

"Yes sir," Sundance said.

"Real agreeable, ain't you?"

"Yes sir," Sundance said.

"You're talking too much," the guard roared, letting his anger loose again. "Break them rocks real small and keep your mouth shut is what you have to do, red nigger. Oh Jesus Christ, red nigger, don't make me mad at you! All you got to do is make me mad and I'll kick a lung out of you. That's hard to do, but I managed it one time."

"Grub's coming up," the other guard called out.

"Red nigger, it's lucky for you I'm hungry," the guard named Joe said. "You was just getting me mad. Now get over there and eat with the rest of the pigs. You got fifteen minutes to down your swill and rest. After that you got to get back here and pay for your crimes all over again. Don't you wish you'd been a good boy on the outside?"

A small hand-cart pulled by a very old and wrinkled trusty creaked up the hill. "Soup's on," the trusty said.

"What's for us?" Joe asked.

"A nice meat stew with plenty of meat in it," the

trusty said. "There's apple pie with cheese on top for dessert. Loads of coffee."

The guards took their stew pot and plates and sat on a rock with their shotguns beside them. Sundance looked at the big chunks of meat that Joe doled out for the other guard. His stomach fluttered with hunger and he longed for a cup of strong black coffee. The trusty took the apple pie, wrapped in muslin to keep off the flies, and handed it to Joe.

Sundance and the other prisoners were lined up at the hand-cart when the trusty came back. "No shoving and no asking for extries," the trusty warned. "You get what you get."

The soup did look like swill; lumps of pork fat floated in the greasy liquid; it might have been anything. When Sundance's turn came, he was handed a tin bowl and a chunk of hard bread. No spoons were provided because a stolen spoon could be sharpened into a weapon, then fitted with a wooden handle and bound with string or wire.

Engrossed in their food, the two guards paid little attention to the prisoners. There was no need, Sundance thought, because the Gatlings would open fire even if the guards were overpowered and taken hostage. The result would be eleven dead convicts, two dead guards; the prison would remain secure. Allowing hostages to be killed was a savage rule, but there was no doubt that it worked.

Myler ate by himself, head bent over his bowl, drinking the rank-smelling soup, chewing on the hard bread. When he finished, he picked out pieces of pork fat with his fingers. Then for some reason he looked up and stared at Sundance, as if he hadn't been aware that a new prisoner had joined the rock gang. His eyes widened and he seemed about to speak when Sundance made a sideways motion with his hand. Myler's body quivered for a moment before it slumped again.

"Come and get your water," the trusty called out, lifting a small keg of water from the cart and setting it down. He took an empty keg from the rockpile and put it in the cart. The prisoners lined up to drink. Myler walked ahead of Sundance, making no sign of recognition, and while they were drinking Joe blew a whistle and ordered them back to work.

"You got one more minute to get your drinking down," he roared through a mouthful of pie. The other guard said something that Joe didn't agree with. "Like hell, Mose! They're in jail, ain't they? Rules is rules and has got to be obeyed."

They toiled through the blistering hot afternoon. Now and then a prisoner asked permission to get a drink of water. Sometimes Joe gave it and sometimes he didn't. The white prisoners got to drink more than the Mexicans or Indians. Myler asked for water and got it. Sundance just worked away, feeling less shaky after the food, bad though it was.

In the afternoon two convicts came up the hill and stood watching them. One was hard-faced, wiry for his age. The other was in his twenties, not as tall as the hard-faced man, but bulging with muscles. Their prison uniforms were new and the shoes they wore weren't jail shoes at all but store shoes, greased and blackened. Old Wade and Mingo, Sundance decided—they had to be.

This was verified when Joe said, "Anything I can do for you, Mr. Bracken?"

Bracken took a handful of cheroots from his pocket and gave two to the guards. He put one in his mouth and Joe lit it for him. Mingo didn't smoke, it seemed.

"Not a thing you can do for me right now, Joe," Bracken said with a patronizing air. "Just came by to pass the time of day." He nodded at Sundance. "This one been giving you any trouble?"

Joe found that funny. "Lord no, Mr. Bracken. You never saw a politer red nigger in your life. "They tell me he's a bad 'un, but he's all sham, I would say. You'd be s'prised how many hard cases turn out to be mush."

"Enjoy your smoke," Bracken said, and it was more than order than a suggestion.

Puffing the cheroot, Joe walked around, glad to be on intimate terms with the boss convict, the man with all the money.

Trailed by Mingo, Bracken strolled over to where Sundance was working. Nothing was said for several minutes. At last Bracken said, "You like this kind of work?"

Sundance let his swing come down; the rock cracked. "Not much," he said without turning his head.

"Not much, *Mister* Bracken," Mingo said. "That's the way you say it."

Sundance started to swing up the sledge and Bracken said, "Whoa, there. You don't have to do that when I'm talking to you. Joe won't mind. It's all right."

Sundance put down the sledge but held the handle with one hand. Joe and the other guard pretended not to notice.

"Want a smoke?" Bracken asked.

"Don't smoke," Sundance answered. "But thanks."

Bracken lit a fresh cheroot from the stub of the other one. "You're more a whiskey man, I hear."

"Won't be much chance of whiskey in this place."

Bracken blew out smoke. He was soft-spoken but Sundance could see how tough he was. Nobody would take him for sixty, though his face was seamed and burned by the desert sun. Under the prison coat he wore a clean white shirt with pearl buttons.

"You can get anything in here if you know the right people," Bracken said. "I'm one of the right people. I'm one of the rightest people behind these walls. They say you've had a lot of experience in hard places. Mexico. Texas. All over. You've done things they said couldn't be done, is what they tell me. Any of that true?"

So far there was no threat in Bracken's voice; that would come. Sundance said, "I've done a few things."

"This one is too modest, Mr. Bracken," Mingo sneered.

Bracken ignored him. "You've done more than a few things," he said. "Maybe you figure to do some more."

"Not in here," Sundance said. "I know when I'm beaten. I'll do my time as best I can."

The other prisoners continued to swing their sledges. On the hill the heat was thrown back by the cliff and their bodies dripped with sweat.

Bracken put his foot on a rock and leaned forward on his knee. "There's more than just doing your time. This is no Eastern jail where you sit in your cell twenty hours a day and sew mailbags. There you can keep out of trouble if you try hard. Here it's different. What has the Actor told you about me? You won't be telling tales out of school. The Actor talks about everybody."

"He says you're a very tough man. Blaisdell runs the prison and you run the prisoners."

Bracken chewed his grizzled mustache. Mustaches were against the rules, but he had one, and it looked like he got to shave every day. His hair, no prison clip, was clean and combed.

"The Actor said right," Bracken said. "Could be that I'll have use for a man of your talents. You've done what couldn't be done, eh?" He lowered his voice. "You think you could break out of here?"

"There's nothing can't be done," Sundance answered. "It just has to be figured out."

Bracken took his foot off the rock and lit another cheroot. His pocket bulged with cheroots. His eyes narrowed. "You think I haven't tried to figure a way out?" The question didn't seem to demand an answer. "I'll have to think about you, Sundance. Maybe you won't have to stay on this rockpile for long. There are other jobs that don't break a man's back. Like I say, I'll have to think about it."

Bracken and his shadow went away and soon it was time to quit work. The sun was going down when Joe blew his whistle and ordered them down to the mess hall for the afternoon meal, which was beans with a few scraps of salt pork. No spoons or forks were issued and they ate with their hands. There were no Gatling guns to cover the men, so guards with shotguns watched them from cat-walks fifteen feet above floor level.

Sundance pushed his way through until he was sitting beside Myler at one of the long tables, which were bolted to the floor so they couldn't be torn up and used as shields against shotgun blasts. The benches they sat on were bolted too. Despite the rules, some of the prisoners were whispering, covering up the sound by rattling their bowls.

The men closest to Sundance and Myler were the Mexicans and Indians from the rock gang. Maybe they could speak English and maybe they couldn't. The Indians looked like Pimas.

"Don't let on you know me," Sundance said in

Apache to Myler. "I'm here to get you out if I can. It's all right if we start talking after a few days. Are you allowed to talk at all?"

"At Sunday service, then when we're exercising later in the day." Myler seemed more interested in his food than what Sundance had to say. "We're not going to break out of here." He began to scrape the bottom of the bowl with his dirty fingers.

"Just hang on," Sundance said. "We'll get out."

One of the Mexicans was paying too much attention; he could be a spy for Tyson. But Tyson would hardly plant a spy on the rock gang. The work was too hard for a man willing to spy on the other prisoners. It was something Tyson might do, just the same.

"What are the chances of getting more of this slop?" he asked Myler in English.

Myler didn't hear or didn't want to answer. The Mexican, the curious one, smiled at Sundance with broken teeth. "You'll get to like it after a while, my friend."

The whistle blew and they were locked up for the night.

Chapter Six

"How are things in the great world outside this cell?" the Actor asked after the door slammed on Sundance and he stretched out on a bunk. Darkness was total after the iron door closed. "They'd let me out if I worked. Tell me what happened?"

Sundance told him about Bracken. "He came nosing around with Mingo. You're right. He has the guards calling him 'Mr. Bracken.' He offered me a smoke."

"You should have taken it," the Actor said. "Tobacco is money in here."

"The guards would have taken it away from me."

"Not if old Wade gave it to you. What did Mingo do?"

"Nothing," Sundance said. "Not after Bracken said he might have use for me. He hinted about breaking out of here. I thought you said he was trying to work a parole."

The Actor chuckled. "They must have turned on him. That could happen. Old Wade's relatives may have decided they're better off with him locked up. Not that he's too locked up. I wish I could be as locked up as he is. Did he threaten you?"

"He said he was boss of the prison."

"That was threat enough. What else did he say?"

"That I might not have to stay on the rock gang for too long."

An exclamation of surprise came from the Actor. "Did he say that? If he wants you off the rockpile he must want something from you, and I don't mean what I was talking about. Old Wade likes them as young as he can get. Whatever it is, you snap it up. Your brains will cook if you stay long on that hill. Next time he offers you a smoke, take it and give it to me if you don't want to trade. Women I don't care about anymore, but I do get a strong craving for a smoke. Do that and I won't forget you."

"If I get a smoke you can have it," Sundance promised before he fell into a deep sleep.

The next day was Sunday and the prisoners, all but the Actor and the men in the punishment cells, were turned out to witness a flogging before they were marched to the mess hall, which also served as Reverend Zimmerman's church.

The man to be flogged had tried to kill another prisoner with a sliver of rock sharpened into a knife. If he had tried to kill a guard he would have been hanged. All the prisoners were assembled at the flogging post when the superintendent appeared, freshly shaved, neat in his Sunday suit and white shirt. It was not his custom to speak to the prisoners; he left that to Tyson, who stood solemn-faced, holding the whip.

The man to be flogged was already in place, his hands stretched high above him and locked into manacles. This was the first time Sundance had seen the guard the Actor called "the broken-backed McDuffie," a man who was just short of being a hunchback. His protruding teeth and weak chin contrasted oddly with a bulging forehead. Now and then he glanced at Tyson as if expecting an order of some kind. None came.

Flicking out the whip to its full length, Tyson bellowed, "After this man is flogged he goes in the Snake Hole. He can tell you what it's like after he gets out. So if any of you scum have knives hid, better get rid of them. No trading, though. The man I catch trading a knife gets twice what this man is getting. That's three dozen lashes for you that can't count."

The lash came down and the prisoner screamed.

Later, in the mess hall, Reverend Zimmerman preached a sermon before they were fed. Sundance remembered the son of a bitch from the cemetery, and in a way his bland, waxy face had less pity in it than the faces of the guards. His black suit was unbrushed and he looked like a man who washed his hands and face and nothing else. Safe from the prisoners, he preached from a catwalk, his shrill, irritable voice echoing in the big silent hall. He addressed them as sinners.

"Woe be to the man without repentance in his heart," he declaimed. "My God is an angry God. He is angry with you because of the vicious crimes you have committed against His law and the law of the land. The Lord could smite you down at this very instant. He does not because He is a merciful God as well as an angry one. Mercy, however, must be earned. You are here to be punished and you shall be punished. Accept your punishment, there is no other path to Heaven. No matter how harsh your punishment seems you must welcome it. In a land less lawful than ours you would be exterminated from the face of the earth. Here things are different. At great expense to the Territory of New Mexico you are fed, clothed, housed. Think of that—remember it—when Satan tempts you to rebel against lawful authority. Your superintendent, Mr. Blaisdell, is the finest man I know. That is why you must obey him and his officers without question . . . ."

They got their food after the preacher blessed them and went away. There was no sign of Bracken or Mingo. One of the benefits of having money was not having to listen to Reverend Zimmerman. For breakfast there was thin porridge, one slice of fat bacon, hard biscuits and watery coffee without milk or sugar.

Sunday fare, Sundance thought. He hadn't been able to get close to Myler, and that was just as well. Myler was in poor shape, mentally and physically, and he wasn't sure he could keep up any kind of pace. It would be different if they could break out, then ride a train or a riverboat. None of that was possible.

After eating, they were locked in their cells for three hours and then released for the two-hour exercise period. On Sunday, the mattress factory and the blacksmith were closed, so the prison was quiet except for the buzz of conversation. After a week of enforced silence, the men were letting off steam. Rumors were passed on and added to on the way. Some new prisoners had come in and were being asked how it was on the other side of the walls.

All the Gatlings were turned on the yard, ready to open fire if a riot started. Hunkered down by himself, Sundance watched the guard towers through slitted eyes. The towers could be reached in darkness, never with the naphtha lights flaring from dusk to dawn. The lights made the inside and outside of the prison brighter than the brightest sun. Each light was independent of the other; knocking out one would do no good. If anything, it would only draw attention. Maybe the Actor was right about all the ways that had been tried over the fifteen years of the prison's life. The Actor had listed them all: disguise, guns carved from wood and blackened, feigned death, the ill-fated balloonist riddled with rapid-fire bullets. One man, a mess hall worker, tried to poison the entire prison staff right up to Captain Tyson. He was hanged for that though no one died.

There had to be something that hadn't been tried. Tunneling wasn't possible because of the solid rock foundation the prison stood on. He turned and looked at the wall that segregated the women prisoners from the men. The women's section was much smaller and took up only a quarter of the total prison space. While he was thinking, he heard the women being let out of their cells. Their shrill, excited voices rose into the air, causing the men to turn their heads with longing or lust. A murmur swept the yard and the Gatling guns turned on their swivels, their snouts depressed to rake the yard with lead if necessary. The noise in the women's yard continued, but the men were silent for a while, then talk picked up again.

Sundance wondered how the convicts with money got to the women. Or did the women come to them? If so, where? There seemed to be only one gate to the women's section and that opened inward from the main prison yard. Instead of being slatted it was constructed of solid iron so the male convicts could not look in. He wondered if there might be a sally port, or postern gate, on the women's side. He could only guess because it hadn't been possible to scout all sides of the prison without being seen from the town on the far side of the river. Maybe the Actor would know. Strangely, though the Actor never left his cell, he seemed to know more about the prison than anyone else. He was like a blind man picking vibrations from the air.

The whistle blew and the men groaned, knowing they

were going to be locked up while it was still daylight. Sunday had its advantages, but the prison shut down early. Sundance was standing outside his cell, waiting for the turnkey to come, when McDuffie came running in his crab-like gait and said, "You follow me. The turnkey knows about it."

McDuffie, moving in his grotesque sideways shuffle, led the way to the end of the central cell block. The door of a cell was open and there was a carpet on the floor and a lamp burning though it wasn't dark yet. Bracken sat at a table drinking whiskey and smoking a cheroot. It was hot in the cell, but it didn't stink like the others. The steel bunks had been removed on both sides, and in their place was a fair-sized platform bed with a mattress and sheets on it. An idiot-faced boy of about eighteen turned from stirring a pot set on a two-burner alcohol stove and stared at Sundance. Mingo was there too, dark-eyed and muscular, dangerous.

"You wanted to talk to me?" Sundance began.

Bracken told the idiot to go and walk in the yard. "They let me have the remaining hours of daylight before they lock my door," he said before knocking back a glass of whiskey. "Be nice if I could keep my door open all night—get some air—but they won't do that even for me. Mingo, make sure McDuffie isn't listening. Watch the door.

"You been thinking about what we talked about?" Bracken went on. "I been thinking about nothing else. The reason? They just turned me down for parole. I thought it was all set. I'd like to get out and see who doublecrossed me."

"Maybe you shouldn't be telling me this," Sundance said.

Bracken shrugged. "You wouldn't run to Blaisdell

with it. He'd probably believe you, but what good would it do? You'd be dead. Even in the Snake Hole you'd be dead and it wouldn't be left to snakes. What I want to know is, do you have a plan?"

"Not yet," Sundance answered. "Anything I come up with may not work. I've never been in this kind of jail."

Bracken's voice remained calm, but the lines in his face deepened. "I can understand you don't have a plan right now. How could you? What I'm saying is you'd better let me in on any plan you make. Otherwise you'll never escape from here. That's right. My boys are going to keep an eye on you, not so it'll be noticed. You're thinking, why don't I make my own plan, or why doesn't Mingo there come up with something? Making plans for jailbreaks is not our line of work. I'd like you to put your mind to it, Sundance. I sincerely mean that."

"What does that mean exactly?" Sundance wanted to know.

Bracken poured another glass of whiskey, then got up and turned off the stove before he answered. "I want a plan," Bracken said. "One that will work, not some notion or daydream. At least I want to *hear* about some kind of plan. What does it mean exactly if I don't hear of this plan? It would mean a number of things. Mingo might have to help you think. You wouldn't like that, but it wouldn't be as bad as the whipping post and the Snake Hole. If you knew my reputation you'd be wondering why I'm talking so polite and reasonable to you. I'm taking the trouble because something tells me you can do it. It kind of surprises me that you're in here in the first place. Another thing: you didn't do a good job of killing that man."

"I was very drunk," Sundance said. "I didn't even set out to kill him. I could hardly stand."

Bracken eyed him. "It's most peculiar just the same. You want to get off the rockpile? Sure you do. I'm going to get you moved to the mess hall. That way you'll get to move about and see things. You'll get more to eat and the work isn't too hard. I want to hear the start of a plan in a few days. It's time for you to be locked in for the night."

Bracken called for McDuffie and he came promptly. "You through with him, Mr. Bracken?"

"He'll be starting in the mess hall in the morning," Bracken told the hump-backed guard. "Captain Tyson knows about it."

"Would you have an extra cheroot?" Sundance said at the door. "It's for the Actor."

"The hell with that mush-mouth," Bracken said.

"The Actor knows a lot."

"Sure. You're right. Take three. I'll be looking in on you, Sundance."

"For God's sake! I don't believe it," the Actor said when Sundance gave him the cheroots. "They smell so good I hardly know what to do with them."

Sundance stretched out on the bank. "Smoke them, Actor. You got them because Bracken thinks together we can figure a plan that will set him free."

The Actor rooted for a hidden match and lit up. "You can't see me, but I practically have tears in my eyes. Old Wade smokes the best. I'd hate to be the one turned that man loose. He's a funny man. My opinion is he's missing a shingle from his top story. He can be quiet and reasonable, then suddenly he goes berserk. Of course he must be mixed up or he wouldn't be a pervert. A fellow that doesn't know if he's a man or a woman has to be confused. How'd you like his set-up? Did you see the idiot?"

"He was cooking," Sundance said. "Mingo was there. Bracken sent him out to see that McDuffie wasn't listening."

The Actor smoked with immense enjoyment. "What a place this is. Perverts, spies, maniacs, all trying to do each other dirt. I'm glad I don't have to leave my little cell. However, giving me these cigars has restored some of my faith in mankind. Let me ask you something. Would you break out if it meant taking Bracken along?"

"You don't include Mingo in that?"

"That depends. Bracken might take him if he's useful, but as we all know, the more men try to escape the quicker they'll be spotted. On the other hand, if enough escape, that keeps the trackers and posses busy. Naturally they have to run in different directions. You didn't answer the question, Sundance."

"I want to get out of here any way I can," Sundance said. "I'll work with Bracken if I have to. He can't be the worst prisoner in the place."

"Pretty much he is." The tip of the cheroot glowed in the dark. "Of the sane men, he's the worst. You can't count the loonies, the maniacs they keep chained up all the time."

The Actor whistled when Sundance told him about the denial of Bracken's parole. "No wonder he's so eager to quit this bucolic spot. I'd hate to be those doublecrossing relatives if old Wade ever makes it back home. It'll be a slaughter."

"I guess it would at that," Sundance said. "Look, Actor, I don't want Bracken nosing around, but that's what he's doing. What do I do? Tell him to go to hell and have that gang of thugs down on me? Besides, he got Tyson to transfer me to the mess hall. I start work in the morning."

"That may mean I'll be losing your company," the Actor said. "The mess hall men are the best treated in the prison. The prisoners try to stay on their good side so they won't do objectionable things to the food. They cook for the guards too. What kind of a cook are you?"

"I can fry meat and boil coffee."

"Elegant." The Actor chuckled. "You'd never get close to that kitchen if old Wade hadn't arranged the move. You won't go hungry, that's for sure. You'll even get to eat the damaged fruit the guards don't want. Fresh peaches, apples, plums. I hardly know what they look like any more."

High on the walls, near yet distant, the guards called back and forth. Wind-blown dust sifted into the cell, and that was all.

"I'll do what I can about getting your food," Sundance said. "While you're thinking about food, spare some time for thinking up a plan that will interest Bracken. I've got to have more time than he's giving me."

Sundance pretended to be asleep so the Actor wouldn't do any more talking. He liked the man in spite of his craziness—and he was crazy, no matter what he said, but his ramblings never led anywhere. Still, he knew the prison better than any man in it, and he knew it in a way that was more valuable than the tough talk of convicts. Bracken was the problem right now, not Blaisdell or Tyson. He figured he could stay out of Tyson's way if he worked hard and broken one of the rules. Of course, there could be rules he didn't know about. Never mind that—at the moment the real threat was Bracken.

He was off the rockpile. How could he get easier work for Myler? One way would be to tell Bracken the truth. The convict boss had all the privileges money could buy; he had nothing to gain by informing to Tyson. A wild story on the face of it, nevertheless it would convince Bracken that he really intended to break out. Any man who deliberately rigged a jail sentence for himself would surely mean to escape. Maybe Bracken would believe him.

Next morning, at five o'clock, he was turned out with the rest of the prisoners. The sky was streaked with red and, as he stood outside the cell, waiting to be marched off, the naphtha lights were turned off.

"You're for the mess hall," a guard shouted. "Get over there and report to the kitchen guard. On the double."

This was the first moment of freedom Sundance had had since he entered the Cage. It lasted for less than fifty yards. The riflemen on the walls watched him until he reached the mess hall and went in by the side door, which opened into the kitchen, a big room with wood stoves line up on one side. The guards' stove and utensils were separate; everything shone. At a table a guard sat with his cap pushed back on his head. On a plate in front of him was a thick ham steak, hard-fried eggs and a pot of coffee. Sundance looked at the coffee pot; he liked hot black coffee more than anything else. Three cooks bustled about.

The guard chewed and swallowed and pointed his fork at Sundance. "The captain says you're going to work here. The captain bosses a lot of things. I boss the kitchen. The guards eat first, so as soon as their breakfast is ready, take it into the mess hall. And look lively. They'll boot your backside if the food's cold. You're dirty, mister. Get cleaned up some. There's a trough outside, see that you use it."

The guard gestured at one of the cooks. "Give the bald Indian some soap and a scrubbing brush. Don't try to run away, or you'll be the cleanest dead man in these walls."

The cooks laughed dutifully and went on with their work. With the stoves going, it was as hot as hell.

Sundance came back cleaner than he had been, and when the food was ready he placed it on a small cart and pushed it into the mess hall. The guards ate in shifts; this was the first. They stared at him as he placed the platters and dishes on the long table where all the guards sat.

"Hey, Briggs!" one man shouted. "Since when you we have to eat food that's been pawed over by a dirty halfbreed?"

Briggs, still chewing, stuck his head in the door. "Captain's orders. You don't like it, go talk to him. You do that, Crump. Besides, the man ain't been pawing nobody's food."

Crump looked at Sundance, trying to find something wrong with what he was doing. "Don't breathe on the food, for Christ's sake. You want us to get sick eating what you spattered on? Answer up, redskin."

"No sir," Sundance said. "I'll turn my head away from now on."

Crump gave a hooting laugh. "I don't believe it. It can talk American. What do you think of that, boys?"

"Pass the God-damned ham and eggs and button up," someone said snappishly. "You got to talk so much this hour of the morning?"

Sundance returned to the kitchen and was told to put more cut wood in the stoves. The names of the cooks were Tompkins, Iversen and Dix. Tompkins, a big-bellied man of about fifty, was in charge. "We already et," he told Sundance. "You can eat what they leave on the platters. There should be coffee left over too."

Briggs, the kitchen guard, took no notice of this.

The prisoners wouldn't be fed until they had worked for two hours. Then Sundance and the assistant cooks would take their food into the mess hall and dole it out.

After the guards trooped out, Sundance ate what was left, wolfing it down, all the time thinking the kitchen guard would take it away from him. The coffee was nearly cold but he drank cup after cup until the pots were empty.

Briggs pushed his plate away and fitted his cap on his head. "Eat your grub in a civilized manner, redskin. This ain't no pigpen. You'll get fed as long as you work here. Don't make no trouble for me, that's all I want."

Belly full and comfortable, Briggs read a newspaper while Sundance scoured fry pans and pots. "Put a shine on them," the head cook ordered. "I want it so a man could shave his face in them things. Then help me get breakfast for them pore prisoners."

Breakfast for the convicts consisted of porridge and hard bread; this wasn't Sunday so there was no fatty pork. Water instead of coffee. There were shouts of "no talking" from the catwalks when Sundance and the assistant cooks trundled in the food. He was surprised to see Mingo sitting with the others. But he didn't touch the bowl that was placed in front of him. The man beside him whispered and Mingo pushed the bowl over to him. For all the guards' warning, the prisoners talked out of the sides of their mouths when they saw Sundance. This wasn't making him any friends, he knew. In just two days he had worked his way from the rockpile to the kitchen, the most coveted job in the place. The work was hard, but the food and the coffee made up for it. Unlike the other convicts, the men in the kitchen were well fleshed out on the leavings from the guards' meals. There had to be some way he could get Myler off the hill; even making bricks would be better than swinging a sledge. He would have to talk to Bracken—no way out of it.

Bracken had given him a few days to make a plan, but what could he say that made sense? The man who killed Mexicans for sport would kill him too if he thought he was lying. Mingo watched him as he worked, and it could be that Bracken hadn't sent him. The brainless strongman probably hated his guts, as the dumb always hate the smart, and the fact that he was in Bracken's good graces, for the moment, was sure to cause trouble.

Sundance would have killed Bracken if it had been possible, but Bracken's thugs always stayed close, if not Mingo, then someone else. Even if he found a way to get the thugs away from Bracken, it would mean killing the idiot pervert too. That was no good: he hadn't come this far to start murdering idiots.

During the morning he worked under the head cook's direction, sweeping and then scrubbing the mess hall. He was finishing up when Briggs, the kitchen guard, shouted that he was wanted in Captain Tyson's office right away.

"That means walk fast or run," the guard yelled.

"Reporting, sir," Sundance said when he got there. The door was open and Tyson was drinking coffee at his desk. He folded a copy of the *Police Gazette* and tossed it into a drawer.

"Get in here," Tyson said, pouring more coffee and dumping in sugar directly from the bowl. "Convicts don't report. They jump when I snap my fingers. Understood?"

"Yes, sir," Sundance said.

Tyson split a match with his thumbnail and began to pick his teeth. "There's something wrong with you, is what I think. You were such a great big fighting man before you came in here. Now you're so polite it makes me want to puke. Why is that?"

"It's the best way to serve my sentence, sir."

There were no guns in the captain's office; none that Sundance could see. Maybe Blaisdell had warned him about being overpowered while he was alone with a prisoner.

"That's a good answer, " Tyson said. "But I don't know if it's the truth. There's something fishy about you and I can smell it. Been a jailer too long. Now another man could say what you just said and I'd believe him like a shot. Not you, though. Why do you think that is?"

"Maybe you're thinking of what I did in the past, sir," Sundance said.

"You can say more than that." Tyson flicked the match and it rang against the brass cuspidor. "I'd like you to say something would take away the twitchy feeling I have about you. Say it."

"Sir," Sundance started. "I know I'm not going to get out of here any way except the main gate. I've been with the military and I know what Gatlings can do. I've been here just a few days but I see how the jail is set up. If I can't break out I'd better make the best of it. What's the good of beating my head against the wall?"

"It looks like you are making the best of it," the captain said slowly. "Yesterday you were sweating your bollocks off on the rock gang, now you're in the kitchen and living high on the hog. Eating high on the hog. It was arranged, as you know. That's beside the point. Why does Wade Bracken have this big interest in you?

You went to his cell. You went because I said you could. You're not what Bracken likes so it can't be that. Talk.''

Sundance said, ''Bracken wanted to know if I was going to make trouble for him. Sir. He said no convict ever did that.''

''What kind of trouble?''

''Any kind, sir.''

''Sort of say it plainer.''

''Sir, he said he knew about my reputation and asked if I thought that would work in here. I said no. I said I just wanted . . .''

Tyson rapped the desk with his knuckles. ''Let's not have that speech over again. I'm tired of listening to it. That's all you talked about, is it?''

''Just about, sir,'' Sundance answered.

''Just about, sir,'' Tyson mimicked, showing signs of anger. ''I think you and Bracken had a lot more to say than that. Did he tell you his parole was turned down?''

''No, sir.''

Tyson slammed the desk with the flat of his hand, making the coffee cup rattle to the edge and fall on the floor. It was tin so it didn't break. Sundance wondered if he'd land in the Snake Hole after they tried to beat the truth out of him.

''I think you better know a few things,'' Tyson said. ''Bracken may be an important man outside these walls. Money, the rest. That helps him in here. You know it and I know it. The hell with that. But when it comes right down to it, any privileges he has can be taken away and he can go on the rock gang if I say so. That's all it takes here—my say-so. Now you're not half—a *quarter* —as important as Bracken and just about anything can happen to you. Mister, if I felt like it I could have you taken out and shot or hung, if I said you tried to attack me. That's the rule here: try to jump a guard—especially the head guard—and you get hung. Maybe you don't believe me?"

"I believe you, sir," Sundance said. "I don't want to get hung or anything else."

"Now you sound like you're telling the truth," Tyson said. He pointed. "Pick up that cup you knocked off my desk."

"You did that real nice," Tyson said when Sundance straightened up. "Always keep in mind I'm the boss of this prison. Bracken may have it soft, but that's just from day to day. Hour to hour, if you like. You're just minute to minute. I'll ask you again. Did you and Bracken talk about anything else?"

"Nothing else, sir," Sundance said. "I'd tell you if we did. I don't want to get on your bad side, sir."

Tyson smiled. "You'll hang if you do. From here on in, I want to know everything Bracken says to you or his perverts. Nothing too small he can say I won't be interested in. You work along with me and you won't be sorry for it. Play smart with me, and you'll die crying for your redskin mammy. Get back to the kitchen and keep thinking about what I said."

"Yes, sir," Sundance said.

Chapter Seven

THE Actor was eating a piece of steak left over from the guards' supper. He took very small bites, chewing slowly, making it last as long as he could. The only light in the cell came from the naphtha lights in the yard. It was hot, but the cell didn't smell too bad because the slop bucket had been emptied, as they all were, at sundown.

"It's like tasting something for the first time," the Actor said. "Or it's like lying with the same woman after many years have elapsed. You aren't sure you know her, but you think you do. Sorry, my friend, I am talking too much as usual."

Lying on his bunk, Sundance said, "Doesn't bother me, Actor."

"You are in a dire predicament, indeed you are," the Actor said. "Between the devil and the deep blue sea is nothing to being caught between Bracken and Tyson. Sorry again. There is no need to tell you that. You asked me to formulate some sort of plan. Well, I have. Do you want to hear it?"

"Anything is better than what I've got."

"Very well then," the Actor went on. "It might even be a good plan, but all I can do is tell you what it is. I can tell you are a man who isn't afraid of much, yet there must be something you fear."

"I'm afraid of being hanged by a hangman that doesn't know how to do it," Sundance said. "Kicking at the end of a rope, knowing what's happening to me while I strangle. I'm afraid of that."

"So would I be," the Actor said. "My plan is based on the fact that everyone is afraid of something. In all of us there is some secret fear that we are reluctant to admit even to ourselves."

"Skip forward a few pages," Sundance said. "This secret fear?"

"I think our superintendent is in mortal terror of losing his other arm," the Actor said. "I don't think he's afraid to die—dying is easy enough—but what if he were left armless, helpless, unable to scratch his head or wipe himself? You went through the usual interview with Mr. Blaisdell. Think of all the precautions he takes against being overpowered by a prisoner. The chair bolted to the floor, the straps, leg-irons, handcuffs. He lost his arm to a prisoner who got the better of him. One from two leaves one. One arm, all he's got. A man who held a pistol on him might be able to walk out of here."

Sundance turned in the half darkness. "But he's ordered the guards to open fire if anyone is taken hostage. That goes for him too."

The Actor laughed quietly. "Very selfless of him, I'm sure. Heroic. But the thing is, would the Gatling gunners really open fire?"

"They have their orders."

"And they have their graft, which is even more important to them. Mr. Blaisdell may not be afraid to die a martyr's death for the sake of his beloved prison. My guess is the guards, especially Captain Tyson, would prefer that he lived. Think of it, Sundance. Tyson would be delighted to see his superior dead if he thought he had a chance of becoming superintendent. There is no chance of that. He can read and write and that's about all. Tyson is next to illiterate, the governor would never appoint him. So what happens if Blaisdell is killed? A new superintendent is appointed, perhaps a man with different idea as to how a prison should be run. A rare man, an honest man, a man who hates graft. Who is to say that he wouldn't kick Tyson and all the others out of here?"

"You've given this some thought," Sundance said.

"Ever since you asked me to think about it," the Actor said. "I'm surprised I didn't think of it before. But I was making plans for myself, impractical plans, plans too clever by far. You are afraid of strangling on a rope, I am afraid of losing my memory. I think I would do anything rather than have that happen. My memory is all I have. I live on it, do you see? As to how you are to point a gun at Mr. Blaisdell, I have no idea. Getting a gun is the smallest part of escaping from here. But say you have the gun and you are alone with our superintendent. The scene is clear in my mind. He stares at the gun and dares you to kill him. It's possible that he longs for the release of death. He reviles you, calls you a dirty halfbreed, etcetera. Then you aim the gun at the only arm he has left and tell him what you're going to do if he doesn't call off the guards and walk through the gate with you. For a moment there is a stand-off, and he tells you to give up the gun because what you're doing is madness and won't work. Then you tell him you won't put just one bullet in his arm but all six bullets in the cylinder. You will blow his arm from his body. Can that be done with six bullets?"

"With less," Sundance answered. "If you put all the

bullets in the same place. Blaisdell was in the army. He'd know that without having to be told."

"Excellent." The Actor was delighted. "So there you have it. Mr. Blaisdell has to bend his rules or face life as a hopeless cripple. Spoon-fed, helped with his calls of nature, unable to unbutton his fly. Yes, and unable to commit suicide unless he eluded his guardians and found a cliff to jump off. You might threaten to shoot off one of his legs."

Sundance smiled at the mild man's ferocity. "The arm would be enough," he said. "Maybe it can be done."

The Actor showed his surprise by gasping. "It was just something to tell old Wade. A bone to keep him from biting."

"It's a good plan," Sundance said. "It could work. The hard part is to get close to Blaisdell."

"Yes," the Actor said. "I think you'll have to betray a few people before you'll be able to do that. That part I leave to you, but I'll think about it too, and . . ."

A snuffling snore announced that the Actor was asleep. Sundance turned on his side and wondered if it could be done. Everything the Actor said was logical enough. A wild plan but one that might work better than, say, seizing the arsenal. It would hold Bracken's interest; that was for sure. Maybe Bracken could get him the gun. It could be that he had one stashed away. But the idea of breaking out with Bracken went against the grain. To help the son of a bitch get free went against everything he stood for, yet there were ways of getting rid of Bracken. That wouldn't be so easy if Mingo came along. Mingo, and maybe some of the others. If Bracken planned to murder his doublecrossing relatives, then he would need a gang. There might be an awful lot of killing before this was over.

Well, after all, killing was his business.

In the morning, on his way to the kitchen, Sundance saw Myler being marched up to the hill with the others. The day's work hadn't started, but he looked ready to drop. In the kitchen the first rush of the morning came with getting the guards' breakfast on the table in time. As fast as the cooks could work, great stacks of pancakes, sausages and fried eggs were prepared and shoveled onto platters. The kitchen guard, first to eat, sat drinking coffee and reading a newspaper, sighing with satisfaction as he forked food into his mouth. Stove lids glowed red by the time the last of the food was placed on the cart and wheeled into the mess hall.

Later, Sundance ate leftover sausages and eggs and waited for Mingo to come around. By the time he turned up, Sundance had washed the plates, scoured the pots and frypans. He was out back collecting an armload of cut wood for the stoves when Mingo came round the corner of the mess hall and stood with a half-smile on his face. He put his foot on the woodpile and wiped dust from his greased boot.

"You got anything you want to tell Wade?" he asked, inspecting the other boot for signs of dirt.

"Tell him Tyson has been coming down hard on me," Sundance said. "Wanted to know why Bracken got me off the rock gang. I'd best talk to Bracken as soon as I can."

"You can talk to me," Mingo said. "Not a thing you want to tell Wade you can't say to me."

Sundance picked up the load of stove wood. "That's not what Bracken said. I've got to get this to the kitchen. Tell Bracken what I said."

He was turning away when Mingo tripped him and he fell against the wall, dropping the wood. When he straightened up there was a chunk of wood in his hand. Mingo looked at it.

"You ain't fixing to hit me with that, are you, half-breed?" Mingo's smile said it couldn't be done. "I can take that away from you and stick it up your glory hole. That turnkey in the kitchen ain't going to get in the way if you have a mind to fight. He's deaf when it comes to what goes on 'round me."

"What about Bracken?" Sundance said. "You want to fight or tend to his business?" He didn't know how much of a match he would be for Mingo, the muscle-bound strongman. Mingo was well fed, didn't smoke, probably didn't drink; there was no fat on his rocklike body. He was young and there was plenty of speed left in him.

"What I do to you won't be fighting," Mingo said. "You'll get the worst beating of your life and you'll take it. Now and then I'll leave off beating so's you can beg for mercy. You'll have to beg real hard before I let you crawl away."

"Sure," Sundance said. "Right now I have to talk to Bracken. You'd better tell him."

"I'll tell him when I feel like it," Mingo said, but Sundance knew that was just a bluff, a way of saving face. Trouble with Mingo was inevitable; all he could do was try to put it off as long as possible.

Mingo went away and it was well into the morning before the kitchen guard told Sundance to go and sit in the mess hall. The hall was empty and no guards patrolled the catwalks high above the tables. In the hall the air was still and hot; old food smells warred with creosote disinfectant. After a while, the main door opened and

Wade Bracken came in. He was alone. Sundance looked at the older man; except for the madness in his eyes, he might have been any quiet, well-off rancher.

Bracken sat on the other side of the table and lit a cheroot. "Mingo said you had trouble with Tyson. That's why I waited till he went into town. What did he have to say?"

Sundance told him.

"It looks like you bother him too," Bracken said. "Just the way you being here bothers me."

They looked up when the guard opened the door from the kitchen and stared at them for a moment. The door closed again.

"You're thinking he'll tell Tyson anyway," Bracken said. "He's taken care of apart from Tyson. Maybe he'll tell him because he's scared not to. Was Tyson all you wanted to talk about?"

Sundance told him everything except rigging the deal with Dobson Getty. "I needed somebody to shoot, so I shot him," he said.

"Like me and the Mexicans," Bracken said. "I needed somebody to kill, so I killed them. You know about that?"

"What I've been told," he said. "My need for someone to shoot was more pressing than yours."

Bracken took no offense. "You got plenty of nerve. Of your brains I'm not so sure. Didn't you know what you faced when you came in here?"

"Not as much as I know now," Sundance said. "You want to hear the rest of it—the plan?"

"I'll hear you out," Bracken said. "Before you start, let me tell you something. If Tyson thinks he can read men, I can read them better."

Sundance made no attempt to embroider the escape

plan, such as it was. "I don't see there's another way to do it," he said. "First I thought maybe we could seize the arsenal and arm all the prisoners. That could be done, but we'd be no match for the rapid-fire guns. They're sandbagged and can be fitted with shields. We might be able to take them, but by then every man in town would be turned out to fight us."

Bracken lit another cheroot. "I had the same idea," he said. "And came to the same conclusion. Yours is a nervy plan, no doubt about that. You're asking me to go in on a plan that depends on what Blaisdell will do. What you figure he'll do."

"I'm not asking you to do a thing," Sundance said. "You wanted a plan. There it is. Take on the Gatlings if you like. Maybe the arsenal can be stormed, but what's to say Blaisdell doesn't have it fused and ready to blow?"

"That would be like the bastard," Bracken agreed. "This getting your friend Myler off the hill isn't such a good idea. It ties you two together, and that's not so good with Tyson suspicious. You'd do better to think about breaking out by yourself. I've seen the man—make it my business to know everybody in here—and he looks half dead to me. I can't see that getting him out will stretch his life much."

"Then let him be buried outside these walls," Sundance said. "Let him know that he isn't going to be dumped in a lime pit like a sick cow. I owe him that much."

"I didn't figure you for a sentimental man," Bracken said. "What's the difference where a man is buried?"

Sundance said, "No difference to me where I'm buried. I don't know how long or short Myler has to live. I knew he was a sick man when I came in here. He deserves a better shake than he's getting. I won't do a thing without Myler."

Bracken's madness surfaced like a gas bubble in a sewer. His cold eyes narrowed and his wiry body quivered with anger. "You don't make any decisions—I do. I been walking soft around you, thinking maybe you got enough sense to know what I'm like. Looks like you don't. I say forget Myler. We'll work out the rest of the plan. Just forget Myler. You got that through your head?"

"It's no good, Bracken. You can have me thrown in the Snake Hole. I know that. Or you can have Mingo and the rest of your bully boys stomp on me. Then what shape will I be in to do anything about getting you out? You're smarter than your trained apes, so you figure out the odds."

Bracken's smile was deadlier than any threat. "You talked to me like that where I come from, you'd be a dead man by now. I could break you here and not leave a mark on you."

Sundance shook his head. "You'd have to kill me," he said. "You may be tough, but I've been through things you can't even imagine. You'd have to kill me."

"Maybe I would at that," Bracken said slowly, watching Sundance's eyes. "There would be satisfaction in that. No profit though. Let me ask you something, Indian. What do you think about me? The things you been hearing about me?"

"No business of mine you like men better than women."

"That's plain enough. You ever did any of that? They tell me the Indians don't make such a fuss about it."

"They don't," Sundance answered. "There are men

like that in every tribe. Not a lot, a few. They let them alone.''

"Like outcasts?"

"No, just different. What about Myler?"

"I'll get him off the hill," Bracken said, calm restored. "You have any idea how you're going to get a gun into Blaisdell's office? Don't even bother thinking about his house. Nobody gets in there, not even Tyson."

"Can you get the gun?"

"The gun's the easy part. That wasn't my question."

"I don't know how I'm going to manage it," Sundance said. "I know I can't carry it in. I'd be searched."

"Not just searched," Bracken said. "You'll be manacled and strapped in that chair like the first time. Maybe you're thinking you can put a gun to Blaisdell's head between his house and office. Forget that too. He always walks with a shotgun guard when he's in the yard. Everybody has to stop what he's doing when he comes through. Make a move in his direction and you get shot. That's the way it's been all these years. Looks like you have a big puzzle to unravel."

"What about the gun?" Sundance asked again.

Bracken smiled. "I have the gun. That's all you have to know for now."

"How many men you want to go along on this?"

"Mingo goes. What you're asking is, does the boy go? He doesn't. What else are you asking?"

"I asked you how many men and you say Mingo."

"One or two other men," Bracken said, getting angry again. "Can I trust them, you're thinking."

"I was thinking," Sundance agreed. "It's my neck too so I say don't trust men that have been here a long time."

"You say. You never did a long stretch. What do you know about it?"

"I was with the army," Sundance said. "For an enlisted man, the army's something like jail. They can do most anything to you if they feel like it. But it's a safe enough life for a man that knows the ropes. So is jail. I can remember a dozen oldtimers always saying as how they'd never sign up for another hitch. But they did, most of them, when the day came to face the civilian world. Convicts are much the same. They've been known to hang back at the last moment, just when you're counting on them to back your play. And they've been known to trade an escape plan for favors in the future."

"You could do the same," Bracken said.

"I could but I wouldn't. I know there wouldn't be any favors. I'd get nothing but killed."

"So you would, Indian." Bracken stood up, ready to go. "I'll get Myler off the rock gang. A mistake, is what I think it is, but I'll get him off. Don't expect to see him in the kitchen. I can't put two men in there. Probably making bricks is the best I can do. Hot work, sure, but he won't have to swing a sledge."

That night the Actor said, between mouthfuls of cold sausage, "I have been mulling over your problem of how to get a gun into Mr. Blaisdell's office and I confess failure. I'm beginning to think it can't be done."

"It can be done," Sundance said.

"But how?" the Actor asked. "You're a stubborn man, but sometimes that isn't enough. I have overworked my tired brain so much it's in need of oiling. The result? Nothing. What do you think would happen if you got your friend Dobson Getty to come forward and explain that the shooting was a fake? How could they keep you here if the victim confesses to fakery? You might have to serve a short sentence for playing fast and loose with the law, but for that they wouldn't keep you here. General Crook's word would carry a lot of weight once he knew you had changed your mind. It's a thought, my friend. Much as I'd miss your company and the food, I'd like to see you gone from here."

"Can't be done," Sundance said. "Getty wouldn't come forward and there's no way I can make him. Besides, we made a deal and I have to stick to it. Another thing. If the truth came out, the Indian Ring would arrange to have me killed rather than have me start up again. Right now they think I'm finished, no longer a threat."

The Actor sighed in the dark. "You have enemies on all sides of you. But you have a friend in me, patricide though I am. Most murderers kill but once. Otherwise they are rather ordinary citizens."

"Would you like to get out, Actor?"

There was a long silence. "Forgive me," the Actor said. "You took me by surprise. It's been so long that I think of escape only as an abstraction. I'm no man of action, Sundance, though I was spritely enough on stage. I'd be an odd addition to old Wade's gang of desperadoes. I know so little about firearms—nothing, in fact. I have fired blank cartridges in the theater. Would that count as experience?"

"Shooting by itself won't get us out of here," Sundance said. "If you want to go, say so."

The Actor's bunk creaked as he propped himself up

on an elbow. "But you don't owe me anything—why?"

"I owe you a few things. The size of a favor doesn't count with me. You worked out a plan, the start of a plan. It's a good plan because it's so simple. That I haven't figured out the rest of it is no fault of yours."

"I'll go with you if you'll have me," the Actor said so quietly that Sundance could barely hear him. "After all these years, to think there's a chance to walk the streets a free man. This place has changed me so much . . . do you think I could get back in the theater? No more juvenile parts of course. After having endured this purgatory I'm sure I could play *Lear* with conviction."

Sundance smiled. "First things first, Actor."

"You think I shouldn't go back into the theater?"

"Might not be such a good idea. Most escaped prisoners get caught because they start doing what they did before."

"Then what are you going to do, my friend? Disregard what I said about resuming my acting career. A flight of fancy, nothing more. I am ready to polish spittoons for the rest of my life if it means my freedom. All I ask is a modest room, a few books, a smoke now and then, an occasional visit to the theater—any theater, and never mind how bad the players. I can't see you doing any of that."

"I'm going to try to clear Myler and myself," Sundance said. "If I can't, then we'll have to go to Mexico and stay there. I've been there before. It wouldn't be a bad life."

"But you'd rather not go?"

"Rather not have to stay."

"I'd stay anyplace," the Actor said. "I don't even mind if I get killed, just so long as it's outside these walls."

Later, with the Actor snoring, Sundance thought, We may all be killed. All it will take is one nervous guard, one guard with a hangover, one guard who hates his wife and wants to kill the world because he can't kill his wife; one guard still nursing some ancient hurt inflicted by Blaisdell. Or it could be a guard, someone crouched behind a Gatling, a man suddenly gone berserk, perhaps not with anger but with the knowledge that he possessed the power to kill. The power to kill was an awesome thing, especially the power to kill legally and with no threat of punishment after it was done. The guards who manned the rapid-fire guns hadn't used them except in practice; firing at the outlines of men painted on boards would hardly satisfy a man eager to experience the real thing.

Sundance turned over on his side, feeling the steel slats of the bunk bite into his flesh. The little air that came through the small square of bars high on the door wasn't any cooler than the fetid air of the cell. On the walls of the prison, the guards on night duty called back and forth. A freight train rumbled over the bridge that separated the prison from the town, and the loud gasping of air brakes sounded before the locomotive started across the trestle, and then the train picked up speed again and passed through the town without stopping. There was a long blast on the hooter—a lonesome sound —and then the train was gone.

In his mind's eye he saw the trainmen—there wouldn't be many on a freight—engineer, fireman, brakeman, one or two others. A few hobos had to be included; they were human beings too. And, thinking of ordinary people, he knew he had to face what he didn't want to face. Bracken and his hidden pistol might be a way out, but was it worth it? To free Bracken wasn't the same as helping to break out a tired old convict like the Actor, who had paid for his crime many times over. That Bracken, if freed, would be killed sooner or later meant very little, since many others would die before some marshal or posseman or bounty hunter put an end to him. He might last for months, even years, and what would be the toll in human misery?

Bracken was something he hadn't figured on. Sure, all prisons had their convict bosses; few had men like Bracken, with his money and his madness. Loosing Bracken on the world would be nothing short of murder, and he couldn't do that even for Myler. So Bracken and his men had to be destroyed, during the escape or later. It was a grim prospect but there was no way out of it.

He wondered how long Tyson would hold off before he got rough. No doubt the graft he got through Bracken's friends made up much of his take. Tyson was a greedy man, but he'd act against Bracken if he felt a threat to his job. Any day now, Bracken might find himself on the rockpile, all his privileges gone, being worked harder than any convict in the Cage. The superintendent might be surprised at the sudden reversal in Bracken's fortunes, but he would not interfere as long as his prison remained secure.

If they managed to walk out with Blaisdell, they would have to hold him until they were out of range of the rapid-fire guns. Bracken would want to hold him longer than that. Bracken would have his own plans for the superintendent, maybe torture but certainly death. If that happened, any attempt to clear Myler would be a waste of time. All the law would know was that he had been a party to a murder.

If captured, Myler would hang, and so, Sundance knew, would he.

Chapter Eight

AFTER Bracken got Myler transferred to the brickmaking gang, he stayed away from Sundance for the rest of the week. It was easier work, although still very hot, but there was plenty of water to drink. Clay and water went into the making of the bricks. The prison had its own deep well and the water pumped up was clean and cold even on the hottest day of summer.

Sundance made no attempt to speak to Myler, in the yard or in the mess hall. Sometimes Captain Tyson walked around followed by McDuffie, who seemed to exist only to carry out the orders of his superior. Otherwise, the routine of the prison was unchanged, one long day following another, burdened with almost unbearable heat.

Twice, Sundance saw the superintendent walking to his office accompanied by the shotgun guard. As soon as he left his house the guard shouted, "Superintendent, attention!" and all work ceased. No one came to attention but everyone remained still until the office door was closed and locked. Then the dull rhythm of the prison picked up again, the slap-slap of the brickmakers mixing water and clay, the thud of sledgehammers on the hill, the pacing of the guards on the catwalks.

Sundance worked and waited for Sunday, the only day the prisoners were allowed to mingle in the yard. According to the Actor, Captain Tyson usually spent Sundays at his house on the other side of the river. It was a little too soon to be talking to Myler; just the same, he had to risk it. Myler had to prepare himself for the escape; he had to convince himself that it was possible to break out of the Cage.

At night he talked to the Actor, but they were no closer to finding a way to smuggle a gun into the superintendent's office. Plans were made and discarded; others were begun. Fired by a determination to escape, the Actor was less garrulous than he had been; gone were all the references to old plays and forgotten players. No longer resigned to his fate, he seemed a much younger man.

"Maybe all I needed was some good food," he remarked. "You think I should send word to Captain Tyson that I'm ready to go back to work? I'm not doing much good in here. For the rest of my time I'll be the hardest worker this prison ever saw."

"It's best you stay here for a while," Sundance said. "Tyson's suspicious enough as it is. If you start acting like a reformed character, it might make it worse."

That wasn't all of it, but he didn't tell the Actor. The man had brains, his talents were unusual. Blaisdell and the prison officials thought him crazy; there seemed to be little violence in his make-up. A plan was forming in Sundance's mind. No, not exactly a plan—an idea.

"You're the boss," the Actor said. "It's funny I should be so wild to escape after so many years. You think they'll chase me hard?"

"You're a convicted murderer," Sundance said. "They'll chase you as hard as they can. What do you figure to do?"

"Play many parts," the Actor answered. "One day I'll be an itinerant preacher, the next a painless dentist with his tools in the pawnshop. In the old days, when I was at liberty, as they say, I tended bar and cut hair. One thing or another, I'll manage. I'm going to fool them, Sundance, I'm going to get away. And now, belly full and peaceful of mind, I must sleep and dream of the names I'm going to use."

Sunday came and Reverend Zimmerman preached another fierty sermon from the catwalk above the mess hall. Two days before, he had read the burial service over the grave of a convict who had killed himself by smashing his skull against a sharp rock. Suicide, the clergyman said, was the most heinous offense against the law of God, for a man who took his own life was guilty of the sin of despair. Only God and the legal authorities who did His bidding on earth had the right to take life. By taking his own life, Reverend Zimmerman declared, the deceased may have thought that he was placing himself in a position beyond punishment. "Little did he realize that he was going to face a much sterner judge than any to be found in the courtrooms of this territory. At this very moment, this misguided man is suffering the torments of Hell and will continue to do so for all eternity. What is eternity? Think of every single grain of sand in the desert as a century and you will have some idea of what I mean. Yet that is just the beginning of eternity . . ."

Later, in the yard, Sundance found Myler sitting in the shade of the prison wall. Tyson had left the prison several hours before. Sundance sat down close to Myler and spoke without turning his head. "How are you holding up, Selden?"

"I'm alive," Myler answered. "I never expected to see you here. What happened?"

"I came to get you out," Sundance said. "You think you're up to it? My plan is for us to head east, far from the river, then try to make it to the border. I have supplies—water, food, guns, money—buried along the route."

"That's for the outside," Myler said, scratching in the dust with a straw. "How do we get there?"

"That's being worked on. I have to know if you're up to it."

"How did you get me off the rockpile?"

"Wade Bracken. He's in on the escape."

"Nice company you keep," Myler said. "You know what he is, what he does?"

It was hard to like Myler, Sundance thought. Half dead, locked up for life, the old crankiness remained. Two and two never made four to Myler. "Never mind about Bracken," Sundance said. "He's useful to us right now. Later we'll see."

Myler was drawing circles with the straw. "Why should I have to escape when I'm not guilty?" he said.

"Nobody in here is guilty," Sundance said, refusing to be angered by the other man's thick-headedness. "That's what they all say. If the court says you're guilty, then you are. I'll ask you again: are you up to it? Make up your mind because there isn't much time. The captain is suspicious. I'm going with or without you."

Myler threw away the broken straw and wiped out his dust drawings with the flat of his hand. "When do we go?" he asked.

"It won't be on a Sunday," Sundance said. "At least, it won't be this time of day on Sunday. I don't want every man in the yard trying to get out that gate. The guards wouldn't let that happen no matter what. A few men might get away from the Gatlings. It might not be us. Apart from that, I don't want to empty this jail, I just want to get you out. Anybody been bothering you since you started making bricks?"

"The other men must know Bracken got me off the hill. Anyway, they've been letting me alone. A few are even wary when they talk to me. It's like they think I'll set Bracken on them."

Sundance saw Mingo watching him from the other side of the yard. Bracken's principal bully-boy was with two other men, both hard looking, one about Mingo's age, the other a few years older. They had dice and they were throwing for something.

"Let them go on thinking you have pull with Bracken," Sundance said. "So you have if he doesn't turn on both of us."

Myler made a spitting sound but didn't spit. "I never thought I'd see the day when I'd be beholden to the likes of Bracken!"

"Let Reverend Zimmerman do the preaching," Sundance said. "Just make your bricks and do nothing to get thrown in the Snake Hole. Tyson hasn't said anything, has he?"

"Not directly," Myler said. "McDuffie came and told me I was off the hill. Tyson walks by without looking at me."

Sundance squinted against the glare; the sun had moved, the shade was gone. Still no sign of Tyson. "Can you take a beating?" he asked. "Not like you've been getting on the hill. I mean from Tyson. It may come to that. I may get the same."

"I don't think there's much more they can do to me,"

Myler said. "If they beat me, they'd have to keep waking me up. There's a limit to how long they could do that."

"Don't die on me," Sundance said. "Let me say it. There's no love lost between us, but we're on the same side. This thing won't work if you keep feeling sorry for yourself. You've been done a wrong. Wrongs have been done to better men than you. Better men than both of us. If you want to stay here and cry in your turnip soup, then go right ahead."

"You're bunked in with the one they call the Actor," Myler said. "A murderer, a lunatic—is he better than both of us?"

Sundance thought of the Actor lying in semi-darkness, reciting all the parts of Shakespeare's plays in his head.

"He doesn't whine," Sundance said. "If we get out of here it will be because of him. Get used to it. The Actor poisoned his father. Makes no difference to me. I don't figure he's going to go on poisoning people to make a living."

"How are my Indians?" Myler asked.

"Crook says they're all right," Sundance said. "He got a good man appointed in your place. Get rid of your hair shirt, Selden. Think of this. You could have been born a black man or an Indian. Or a halfbreed like me."

"Now who's whining?" Myler turned his head to watch for Sundance's reaction.

Sundance looked at this man with so many good intentions and so few friends. "We all start out by blaming the world for what we are. But most of us, if we're smart, get over it."

"I won't break if Tyson beats me," Myler said. "You can depend on that."

Sundance was well away from Myler when the inner gate opened and Tyson came into the yard. He stood for a moment with a cigar in his mouth, rolling it between his thick lips, then he spat it out. Prisoners looked from Tyson to the smoldering cigar, ready to scramble for it as soon as Tyson walked on. Smiling, Tyson placed his boot on the cigar and ground it into the dust. He kept on moving his foot until the cigar was nothing but shreds. The wind caught the tobacco fragments and blew them away.

McDuffie scuttled across the yard to greet Tyson, but instead of talking they went to the captain's office at the end of the cellblock. The crook-backed guard was going to make his report to his master. Sundance waited, expecting trouble, but none came.

Another hour was left before they would be locked in their cells for the night. That was what they all hated: being penned up with the sun still shining. It meant a long, hot, restless night before they were turned out at five the next morning. The guards hated Sunday afternoons because the routine of the prison was broken; all the men were together and it wouldn't take much to start a riot. If that happened, the Gatlings would start firing and they wouldn't stop until the yard was piled high with bodies.

Thirty minutes were left when Bracken strolled into the yard, nodded to Mingo and the others, but sat in the shade by himself and smoked a cheroot. A few convicts came close, smiling uncertainly, probably asking for favors, Sundance thought. Bracken waved them away and they went, some still smiling, others with disappointed faces, but all afraid of him.

Sundance sat on his heels a distance from Bracken and nothing was said for a while. Overhead the sky was blue and free of clouds and a hot wind blew from the desert, raising tiny whirlwinds of dust in the yard. A train crossed the railroad bridge and the faces of the men turned toward the sound.

"You figure it out yet?" Bracken asked.

"Not so far," Sundance answered. "But you better get the gun to me. It won't be long before Tyson makes a move. If that happens, you can forget about breaking out of here."

"I'll still be boss of this prison, no matter what Tyson does."

"Not if you're on the rockpile or in the Snake Hole. What can you do about it—complain to Blaisdell?"

"I could get Tyson killed," Bracken said.

"Probably you could," Sundance said. "Then you might get someone worse than Tyson, smarter than Tyson. What about the gun? We may have to move fast and there won't be time for passing messages back and forth."

Bracken tapped ash from the end of his cheroot. "It took a lot of work to get that pistol. Guard was left a small ranch by his dead brother. What that pistol cost me was enough to re-stock the place with fat cows. Now I'm supposed to turn it over on your say-so?"

Sundance feigned impatience. "What the hell good is it if you don't give it to me?"

Bracken's mouth tightened. "It's a new Colt Sheriff's Model .45 with a short barrel and six cartridges in the cylinder. It belongs to me. I have it. A gun is power, Indian. I can take my own life with it. That's one way out of here. I can kill Tyson or Blaisdell. I can kill both of them if I get them together. I can kill you if I feel like it."

A silver thread of saliva hung from the corner of

Bracken's mouth. Guessing, Sundance said, "That's whiskey talk, Bracken. All right, you gun down Blaisdell in the yard and the Gatlings cut you to stew meat. You've got six pills in that Sheriff's Model. That's all, not much."

Bracken turned his head to stare at Sundance. No prisoner did that. You didn't do that, not with guards watching all the time. So he was drunk, Sundance knew.

"It's the feel of the pistol gives me comfort," Bracken said. "In the dead of night when I can't sleep I like to slip my fingers around the smooth walnut butt of that new forty-five and know there's something I can depend on. I rest my first finger outside the trigger guard because I might get sleepy with the contentment of having that iron in my hand. That's a precaution in case I'd get vigilant in my sleep and shoot maybe at what might be attacking me . . . ."

"Bracken," Sundance said. "What about the gun?"

"I'm carrying it," Bracken said, smiling. "In the waistband of my trousers. It's not going to fall, Indian, because I get to wear a belt. When Tyson walked by I could have dropped him like a stone."

"And get dropped yourself."

"Sure. That's it."

"When do I get the gun?"

Bracken sneered openly. "That all you know how to say? Is that what they taught you at the mission school? Was there a pretty schoolmarm and did you get all horny looking at her?"

Sundance got to his feet. "The deal's off, Bracken. You break out any way you can. Count me out of it."

He turned as if to walk away, knowing that he might get a bullet in the spine. Then the rapid-fire guns would start hosing the yard with bullets.

"You think you can just walk away from me?" Bracken snarled, climbing to his feet. "Go on, Indian, try it. You got the nerve, you try it."

"We'll both be dead in a minute," Sundance said. It was more truth than bluff."

"Hold on there," Bracken called after him. "Come on back and I'll give it to you."

Sundance turned. "How?"

Bracken said, "Soon as I throw some smokes out in the yard. When I'm raising my hand to throw you take the pistol. The guards are used to me tossing the men a few smokes. Make it fast and smooth, Indian. You lose my new gun and you'll be sorry for it."

By the time the men scrambled to get the cheroots the Sheriff's Model .45 was covered by Sundance's shirt. Bracken walked past, nodding to the prisoners. Sundance waited for something to happen. It seemed incredible that the switch had been made so easily. Walking across the yard, waiting for the lock-up whistle to blow, he felt sure it had been spotted by someone. If they caught him with the forty-five he would be flogged and thrown in the Hole with the snakes that crawled in or were thrown in by the guards. The flogging wouldn't be as bad as the Hole. Without conceit, he knew he was a very tough man. Even so, he was just a man, and there were limits to what a man could take. He kept on walking with his arm pressed against his side. If the gun fell at his feet he would try to grab it up and put a bullet in his head. He wasn't like Bracken and he wouldn't try to kill some guard as a last gesture of defiance. He had no urge to kill anybody.

The whistle blew and a dull, hopeless murmur of

complaint ran through the men in the yard. In the towers the Gatling guns racketed on their swivels. The whistle shrilled again and the men moved toward their cells.

The dead weight of darkness pressed down on the Cage. Wind driven sand sifted through the bars at the top of the door. At the end of the cellblock someone began to sing and there were roars of complaint from men trying to hide in sleep.

"You have the gun," the Actor said. "At least that's a start."

The singing started again and it ended with a scream. Sundance was working on one of the bullets from the forty-five, trying to get the lead slug out so he'd be sure it was backed by real powder. The guard who provided the gun might be a man with a peculiar sense of humor.

He got the slug loose and the powder in the shell tasted right, so it wasn't likely that the others had been spiked. He worked the slug back into the shell and crimped it tight with a sliver of rock. Bracken hadn't been lying: the Sheriff's Model was new and ready to fire.

The Actor said, "That man, the songbird who wasn't appreciated by his cellmates, is dying of slow consumption. Different from the galloping kind. But it carries you off just as surely. We have all the diseases here save cholera. We had it many years ago and it finished off about half the population. Men dropping like flies all over the places. Stuff pouring out of them, one end of the body or the other. Worse than dysentery. All the water goes from the body. You lose pounds in a few hours. A man can lose half his weight in a week. You ever been through cholera, Sundance?"

Sundance put the pistol against the wall under his bunk. "One time in Mexico," he answered. A thought stirred in his head. "I got the feeling of it, but I didn't get it. Hundreds died."

The Actor shifted his weight in his bunk. "I was lucky," he said. "Passed me by. But I did feel the Angel of Death hovering close. The angel flew right down and lighted beside my bunk and said he to me, 'Are you scared, Mr. Maitland?' and I said, 'Not too scared, Mr. Angel, but I'll go with you if you like.' "

"What did the angel say?" Sundance asked.

" 'All I want is them that's scared,' said the angel to me." The Actor's bunk creaked with his laughter. "Must have been a down-home angel to talk like that. But I swear to you I did hear the rustle of his heavenly wings. And I wasn't drunk at the time. How could I get drunk in here? I wasn't scared but Mr. Blaisdell was. Oh lord, how that man was scared!"

"You said Blaisdell didn't scare."

"Not for himself, I think. Though it would seem to me that any man who isn't terrified of cholera isn't sensible. I wasn't sensible at the time I'm talking about."

That was it, Sundance thought—the threat of a cholera epidemic. Bubonic plague was worse but far from common, and usually it came from the bites of rodents. Smallpox hadn't been much of a threat for years. The cholera outbreak in Chihuahua had been very bad, although some of the oldtimers said it was far from the worst they had seen. He remembered how the fires of green wood had smoked night and day. The Mexicans believed that smoke acted as a purifying agent. There was an army doctor named Quintana who got very angry about the smoke and said it didn't do one damned bit of good. The doctor died too, and the townspeople said his death was a judgment—he should not have been so irreverent. Day and night the corpses, the living skeletons drained of their fluids, were trundled out to the burying ground, for they buried the dead and the near-dead in the same pits. Hundreds died; at least half the town.

"You remember how it looked when they had cholera here?" Sundance asked. "The way men looked, how they behaved?"

"How can I not remember?" the Actor said. "Men died so fast they stopped burying the bodies in lime and burned them. For a time it looked like Blaisdell would be superintending an empty prison, then the cholera stopped, the way it does. I have to say this for Blaisdell: he didn't get rattled like Tyson and the other guards. The guards tried to quit and run away from here. That's when Blaisdell ordered the few loyal men to open fire with the Gatlings if any guard made a move toward the gate. A man of great civic spirit, our superintendent is. Didn't want the cholera to spread through the town and the rest of the territory. The governor gave him a commendation for that. Why all the interest in cholera, my friend?"

"You're going to come down with cholera," Sundance said. "The worst case of cholera you ever saw. This won't be Shakespeare, but you'll be acting for your life. Tomorrow night, after they lock me in, I'll start hollering that you have cholera. That should bring Blaisdell. You say he has nerve. Let's hope he has. Tyson and the other guards will hang back if what you say is right. Blaisdell won't come into the cell with me in it. I'll be ordered out so he can look at you. Nerve or no nerve, I'm betting he won't get too close to you."

"Aha," the Actor said. "Meaning I won't be searched. I'll hold the gun on him and you come back in."

"Then we talk terms," Sundance went on. "He'll try a bluff till I tell him he's going to lose the only arm he's got. Can you do it, Actor? No hard feelings if you say no."

"You couldn't keep me from doing it," the Actor said, rubbing his hands together like a hungry man ready for Sunday dinner. "By God, sir, you're going to see a performance tomorrow night! I'm used to this heat but I'll work up a drip sweat by the time Blaisdell comes around to play Florence Nightingale. I'll be the sickest man in existence. How to handle the pistol worries me a bit. Do I cock it or what?"

"Bring it out with the hammer back," Sundance said. "I'll show you how it's done. Bring the hammer back in one firm motion. It's a new gun and there won't be any trouble. Once the hammer is back, keep your thumb away from it, your finger resting lightly on the trigger. Don't aim it at Blaisdell's face. Too small a target even at that distance. Point it at his chest and tell him to stand still. Sing out when you have him covered. Look fierce so he'll know he can't talk you out of it."

The Actor laughed quietly. "I'll look as fierce as Othello," he said. "And there's no man living that can out-talk me. We'll be taking Blaisdell along with us?"

"Till we get clear," Sundance said.

"Old Wade will kill him," the Actor said. "You know that as well as I do. Might I suggest a sensible doublecross? Leave old Wade and his thugs locked in their cells. They'll be locked in the same time as you are. There's no way they can get out."

"I thought of that, Actor. But the only sure way to handle Bracken is to kill him. To leave Bracken behind alive is to guarantee trouble in the future. I have better things to do than wait for him to show up a year from now. Five years from now. Whenever. You think I'm wrong?"

The Actor said, "Far from it. The man is crazy and he'd find a way to escape. My friend, when I get outside these adobe walls I am going to disappear. Wherever I go—and it will be far—I am going to be a model citizen. No spitting on the sidewalk—not that I've done anything so unsanitary. I may even join some undemanding church. I favor the Unitarians, better still, the Society of Friends. It would be distressing if old Wade were to appear at a prayer meeting carrying a sawed-off shotgun." The Actor paused. "When are you going to kill him?"

"As soon as he steps out of his cell."

"That's the ticket. Then we lock up the guards."

"You know where the Mexican tracker lives?" Sundance asked, thinking of the man called Esteban Zorrilla. He hadn't seen him for days.

"The greaser has a small place on the other side of town," the Actor said. "Raises goats, I believe. Blaisdell pays him a regular salary, but it's not enough to live on. Too bad you can't kill him too."

"You've been in jail too long, Actor. I can't kill a man just for doing his job."

"He'll be coming after us."

"So he will. I'll kill him if it keeps us from being killed. That hasn't come yet. Maybe it never will."

"I like an optimist," the Actor said, turning over on his side. "Think of it: in less than twenty-four hours we'll be free men, or we'll be dead."

Chapter Nine

SUNDANCE looked at the rising sun as he walked across the yard to the kitchen. The naphtha lights went out before he reached the mess hall; they would be flaring again by the time he made his move. He felt a great lifting of his spirits as he thought of freedom: a sound horse under him, the cold, clean air of the desert just before first light. He knew they might not make it, but he didn't care. "Live free or die" was a well-worn phrase, yet it had special meaning for him now.

Today, he would have to be careful not to do anything that would bring Tyson down on him. Wanting the hours to pass, he forced himself to be patient. No matter what happened, he had to get through the day. This was the only chance he would get.

The guards came and went and he ate what they left. Briggs, the kitchen guard, seemed to be watching him, but he couldn't be sure. Twice he went out to get wood for the stoves and Briggs followed him, standing by while he loaded the wood. That would be Tyson's doing. He was being watched, all right.

He hoped Bracken would stay away from the mess hall for the rest of the day. The plan itself was simple, but anything could happen before sundown. He knew he could depend on the Actor; the man was a windbag, yet there was a core of strength in him. About Myler, he wasn't so sure, for the simple reason that he didn't know the man. Would he go to pieces when he had to walk out under the muzzles of the rapid-fire guns, not knowing when one of the Gatlings would cut loose? And later, in the desert, would he be able to take the strain of being hunted by men and dogs? There were no answers, just questions.

At noon a shout came from the mess hall and Briggs went to see what it was. "The captain wants you," he told Sundance when he came back. "Is there fresh coffee? It better be fresh or he'll make you dance."

Sundance took the pot of coffee into the mess hall, hot and dark, empty except for the captain. "You're getting to be a good waiter," Tyson said. "It's all right. You can sit with me. Sit, Indian. I'd like word to get around that we're friends."

Sundance sat on the other side of the table.

"You ought to have brought a cup for yourself," Tyson said. "But I guess you get plenty of coffee on this job. How's the food?"

"Very good, sir."

"Work not too hard, is it?"

"No, sir."

Tyson said, "I like a man that knows when things are going good for him. The only trouble is, things can be good one day, rotten the next. So rotten they stink. On the other hand, the good things a man has can get even better. Now take a man like yourself. Right smart, from what I hear. Can read and write as good as any white man. Better than some I know. Now here in this prison we have a lot of prison-made goods. We can't use all the bricks we make, so we sell them. Then there's the mattress factory and the smithy. Mattresses, horseshoes, hinges, nails. We plane lumber here, even sell crushed rock to the county for the roads. Books have to be kept so we know how much money we're making. You ever keep books?"

"No, sir," Sundance answered.

"They tell me a man can pick it up in no time," Tyson said. "Specially a smart man like you. It's the best prisoner job there is. A man has that job keeps his hands clean, has a little office all to himself. In that job a man gets to work close with me so we can work out a few things. There's a few dollars and more than that for a man I can trust. On the other side of that wall there's women. Don't tell me you wouldn't mind a little of that?"

"No, sir," Sundance said.

Tyson leaned forward. "You want the job I'm talking about?"

"Yes, sir," Sundance said.

"Tell me what Bracken's up to. That's all you have to do to get it. Don't talk yet because you might not say the right thing and then I'd get mad at you. So you can have it easy or hard. Facing you, if you don't work for me, is the flogging post, the Snake Hole, maybe the hanghouse." Tyson snapped his fingers. "Like that you could be dead. You had a parley with Bracken yesterday. What did he say?"

Not so many hours remained till sundown. It can't go wrong now, Sundance thought. "Bracken wants to figure a way to escape," he said.

Tyson slammed his fist on the table. "Damn you to hellfire! I know that's what he wants. What the hell do you think every man in here wants?"

"Bracken thinks I can figure a way out of here," Sundance said. "He knows I had some kind of reputation before I came in here. He wants to use the things I can do. That's the truth, sir."

Tyson said, "Some of that is the truth. Bracken wanting to use you is true. Stop dodging around. I told you before I could flog the right answers out of you."

Sundance kept his voice level. "Then why haven't you, sir?"

Tyson lowered his voice. "I think I'm going to need a tough man among the prisoners. Bracken doesn't know it yet, but he's finished here. Give a man an inch and he takes an ell. Bracken's taken a lot more than that. Now he thinks he owns the prison, even talks back to me. To *me!* I can tell you the straight of it because there's nothing you can do. My arrangement with Bracken worked all right for a long time. It doesn't work now. I'm going to get rid of him, but that leaves a hole. You're going to fill it. You're going to boss the prisoners with my backing. I want to know everything that goes on. You know *why* you're going to do as I say?"

"Why, sir?"

"I'll kill your friend Myler if you don't."

"No friend of mine, sir."

"Is that so? Last night I looked at Myler's file. Your name isn't mentioned. I think maybe it should be. Myler was an Indian agent for half his life. You've been fighting for the Indians just as long. What's between you and Myler, is what I want to know."

"Nothing, sir," Sundance said. "Fighting for the Indians wasn't what sent me here."

Tyson smiled, thinking he had his man cornered. "But you do know Myler?"

"I know most of the Indian agents, sir. Myler was a good one, but I never liked the way he handled his job. I haven't seen him for well over ten years. Could be as long as fifteen."

"Myler said the same thing late last night," Tyson said. "Did I beat him hard? you're asking yourself. Not too hard. A stronger man I would have beat harder. But your friend kept passing out on me. You still say he isn't your friend?"

"Not a friend, sir."

"Then you don't care if I kill him? Or if he dies? Comes to the same thing."

To ask mercy for Myler would be to give everything away. Tyson wasn't an intelligent man, but he was cunning. He was as much a criminal as any prisoner in the Cage. Just the same, he knew his stinking job, which was to break men who refused to bend. It was well past noon; time was getting short.

"Do what you like, sir," Sundance said. "I knew Myler a long time ago. This is now. He killed a man and that's why he's here. He'll have to do his time like the rest of us."

Tyson pushed his cup away from him. "Why were you talking to him in the yard? For men that aren't friends, I hear you talked for a while. What about?"

"I wanted to know if he had any friends trying to help him on the outside. A reduction in sentence. Maybe a pardon. I thought his friends might be able to help me. He said he had no friends and didn't want to talk about it."

"Myler wasn't half as free with his words when he talked to me," Tyson said. "He said his mind was wandering and didn't recall what was said. I couldn't shake him on that. Was that what you told him to say?"

"No, sir," Sundance said. "Listen, Captain, I'll work for you, but you've got to keep Bracken and

Mingo in line."

"Don't be telling me my job," Tyson said, but there was no real anger in his voice. "Bracken and Mingo will go in the Snake Hole this very day. The rest of his whitehats will start breaking rocks."

"Might be better if you didn't do that, sir. It will cause a great commotion. The whole place will get jittery, guards as well as prisoners."

"Let it," Tyson said. "Maybe you're right, though. We'll let it ride for now. Just you keep me informed. Play false with me, Indian, and maybe I'll give you to Bracken and his boys. Then I'll finish off the lot of you."

A mosquito buzzed close and landed on the back of Tyson's hand. He slapped it dead and inspected the smear of blood. "There won't be that much juice left in you if you play false with me. Do right by me and you'll have a firm friend."

Tyson went out, humming *What A Friend We Have In Jesus*.

Sweeping out the mess hall, with the doors open, Sundance saw Blaisdell walking to his house accompanied by the shotgun guard. The superintendent's habits were fixed. At seven in the morning he went to his office; at one o'clock he went home to have lunch, allowing himself exactly an hour. Sundown saw him back in his house, where he remained until morning. A strange man, Sundance thought; he seemed to have no real part in the life of the prison.

The Actor was right: everything depended on what Blaisdell would do when the gun was pointed at him. Would he throw himself at the Actor, hoping to overpower the weaker man, or would he hesitate just long enough to make the escape become a reality? Sundance was sickened by the web of deceit in which he was caught. Some of it was of his own making. All his life he had tried to live with honor; now he was mired in lies and betrayal. Bracken's gun might get him out of the Cage, yet he was forced to betray the man. But was that the right word? After all, betrayal meant the breaking of trust. He had given his word to Bracken. Could he justify his betrayal by arguing that he had given his word under the threat of death? The hell with it, he thought. Don't fight something you can't beat.

He could see Myler from the door of the mess hall. His movements were slower than they had been on the rockpile, mixing clay and water like a man in a dream, and it was likely that he would have to rope Myler to a horse before they left the prison. The stables were behind the blacksmith shop. Good horses, he figured.

They would have a fair start with all the guards locked up. The big lights would have to be left burning, but even then some nighthawk from the town might notice that there were no guards on the walls or in the towers. For sure the guards would set up a hollering as soon as they were gone. Maybe the prisoners, crazed with rage and frustration, would do the same. The noise was bound to be heard, so maybe they wouldn't have such a good start after all.

He was thinking too much, Sundance realized; prison changed everyone. He hadn't been there very long, but it was altering the way he thought. Some of it was caused by degradation, by having to sit still and to say "Yes, sir" and "No, sir" to Tyson when his natural instinct was to beat him to a pulp. Anger could have no meaning for him, not in the Cage. The break was set for sundown, and that was that.

Once, during the early afternoon, he saw the Mexican tracker Zorrilla. The guards let him in to the yard and he went to Blaisdell's office. He didn't have his dogs with him and there was no gun in his holster. A solemn-faced man in his late thirties, he spoke to no one, waved to no one. He had the slightly springy walk of men who follow leashed dogs; an energetic tireless walk. A few minutes later he left the prison. Maybe Monday was payday, Sundance thought.

It got to be three o'clock and he wondered how the Actor was doing with his preparations for the big scene. The sun was merciless and there was no wind. All the cooking was done, though some of the guards ventured into the kitchen now and then, to scrounge up coffee or something extra to eat. There was a locked zinc cabinet where food was kept for the guards: cold fried chicken, ham and country sausage. One guard, a tow-headed young man with a twitchy smile, asked Briggs if he'd heard about this method of hanging they were trying out back east in Connecticut.

"It's supposed to be more humane," the guard explained to Briggs, who hadn't heard of it. "Instead of dropping them through the trap, they jerk them aloft by a rope worked by a spring. Up the condemned man goes and his neck is broke rightaway."

"It'll never catch on," Briggs said.

Now only the stove on which the guards' food was cooked remained burning. After lock-up time, if the guards wanted food, they had to cook it themselves. There was a wall clock in the kitchen. Another hour, Sundance thought. Sixty minutes to freedom—or death.

He busied himself with the last of his work, scouring pots with a wet rag dipped in sand, then washing them off under the short-handled pump. Briggs was yawning, sated with food, sluggish from lack of exercise.

In a while the whistle blew and Briggs got up from the table, still yawning. "That's it for today, boys. What's for breakfast, Dix?"

"Steak and eggs, Mr. Briggs," the cook said. "Course you can have anything you fancy. Man had the job before you was a Scandihoovian and used to ask for fish. Wanted sea fish, but had to make do with river cat. No bother to fry you up a big mess of cat."

"I'll think on it and let you know in the morning," Briggs said. "On your way, boys, and don't none of you run off during the night. River cat in a light batter wouldn't be bad."

Here goes nothing, Sundance thought as he walked across the yard to stand in front of his cell. The sky was dark red and the lights were on, lights so bright that they threw no shadows. Cell doors were slamming all over the prison. Sundance waited while a guard moved down the line of cells to where he was. A whisper came through the bars. It was the Actor. "When do I start?"

"Right now," Sundance said, and the Actor let out a howl that echoed off the walls of the prison. It got louder, rising to a scream. It stopped and started again, but the guard did nothing until he got to where Sundance was standing outside the last cell in the row. He rattled his keys while the howling went on.

"He's going crazy in there," Sundance said.

"He *is* crazy," the guard growled, fitting the key in the lock. The door swung open. "In you go, Indian. You can be crazy together." The guard pushed Sundance into the cell and slammed the door. Then he went away whistling.

"You're doing good," Sundance whispered. "Keep it

up, then I'll take over."

The Actor's voice was raised in a series of howls that brought no immediate results, then the other prisoners in the cellblock began to yell back, some kicking the doors of their cells. In a while they were joined by prisoners in other parts of the prison. Soon there was the shouted warnings of the guards as they moved from one cell block to another, kicking on the doors from the outside while the prisoners kicked back from inside. Sundance heard the guards coming.

"Cholera!" he shouted. "This man in here has cholera! Let me out of here! He's sick and crazy and he has cholera!" Sundance pounded on the door with his fists. Then he raised himself until he could see through the bars. "Cholera!" he screamed in what he hoped would be taken for mindless panic.

There were two guards and they stood well away from the door. "What the hell are you yelling about cholera?" one of them said. "You and that crazy bastard is raising the whole prison. Whack his head aginst the wall and go to sleep."

Sundance pounded on the door. "I don't want to touch him! He's wet all over, puking and shitting. I know what cholera looks like, stinks like. We'll all die if you don't get rid of him. You stupid son-of-a-bitching turnkey, I'm telling you he has *cholera!* You don't believe me, open the door and take a look."

The two guards moved back even more; in the glare of the lights their faces were stiff with fright. Sundance yelled at them, but they ignored him and began to whisper. The Actor, shaking with silent laughter, whispered too. "You should have been on the stage," he said.

By now the entire prison was aroused and the dread word "cholera" was passed from cell to cell. The whispers turned from murmurs to wild yells of panic. Even the guards on the walls took up the cry and shouted questions to the men in the yard.

Suddenly, the two guards outside the cell broke off their parley and walked away quickly. In the middle of the yard they were met by Tyson and there was another whispered conference. One of the guards took hold of Tyson's arm and pointed at the same time. Tyson pulled away, warning the guard to keep his distance.

"Scream, Actor," Sundance said, kicking the door again.

Watching Tyson, Sundance saw him turn. Someone was coming; it was Blaisdell and he was struggling into the coat of his grey suit. Tyson pointed and for a few minutes their voices were locked in furious argument. It ended when Blaisdell took the cell key from the guard and motioned Tyson to follow him. The two guards came, too, and Blaisdell told them to hold their shotguns at the ready. One had a dark lantern.

"Unlock the door," Blaisdell commanded. "Cover me is all you have to do. Open the door and get out of the way if you're so afraid."

Tyson hung back. "Don't go in there, sir. I'll get a prisoner to look in there. We can burn sulphur candles and brick up the door."

"You fool," Blaisdell snapped. "The halfbreed's been in there since he came here. He's been in the kitchen after that. If he's infected, so is the whole prison. Now hand me that light and open the door."

The door swung open. Blaisdell lifted the slide on the dark lantern and for a moment Sundance was blinded by the light. A revolver stuck out of Blaisdell's coat pocket, but he couldn't hold the lantern and the gun at the same time. As the door opened, Tyson stepped back. So did the guards, their faces glistening with sweat.

"You go outside," Blaisdell said to Sundance. "Stand away from my guards and keep your hands behind your head. Be quick about it, they have orders to shoot."

Before he went out, Sundance turned to look at the Actor huddled by the side of the slop bucket, no longer screaming but soaked through with sweat. It ran down his face and dripped from his chin. His eyes rolled and his body shook. "I'm not sick, Mr. Blaisdell," he said, holding up one hand against the light. "Old malaria, sir. I won't die of that, will I, sir?"

"Stand right there," Tyson ordered when Sundance came out. "By the door and don't make a move."

There was a muffled cry from the cell and Sundance went in before the guards could shoot. He turned and said, "The Actor is holding a gun on Blaisdell. Fire at me and he'll die the same time. You got him, Actor?"

"Got him," the Actor said.

And he had, for the moment. The Actor was up off the floor and the Sheriff's Model was steady in his hand. The hammer was back. Blaisdell still held the dark lantern and Sundance took it away from him. But first he took the revolver from his pocket. He checked the loads while the Actor watched Blaisdell. "We're going out," he said. "Tell Tyson we're going out and you're coming with us."

Blaisdell's reaction was predictable. "You're going nowhere. Kill me if you like. I don't give a damn what you do. Kill me and then you'll have the Gatlings to deal with."

Blaisdell's gun was a double-action Colt .38. Sundance held out his hand and the Actor gave him the chunky .45. "Tell Tyson we're going out or I'll blow your arm from your body. You'll get all six bullets in the same place, Blaisdell. You want a minute to think on that?"

Blaisdell's face twitched. "That will just get you killed. If you're so brave, why don't you kill me, you halfbreed mongrel? You brown-faced scum, you don't have the nerve to do anything!"

Sundance felt no anger. "How much nerve do *you* have, Blaisdell? Make up your mind and while you're about it, think of the years ahead. How much work is there for jailkeepers missing both arms?"

"What's going on in there?" It was Tyson.

"You want a count before I start shooting?" Sundance asked. "I guarantee I won't kill you. If you lose the arm we'll have to use the bullets in the Actor's gun on ourselves. But you'll be worse off. You want to be an armless hero, now here's your chance."

Sundance raised the heavy Sheriff's Model and pointed it at the place where Blaisdell's arm joined the shoulder. For an instant he thought it wasn't going to work, then Blaisdell's body sagged and he said in a dead voice, "I'll do what you say."

Sundance said, "Tell Tyson there's to be no shooting. All the guards are to assemble in the yard so they can be locked up. Tyson and two other men are to fetch six horses from the stable. Winchesters in every boot. Water that isn't poisoned in fifteen canteens. You'll get to drink the water first. You just make sure it isn't poisoned or salted. Six handguns. Ammunition. A big sack of canned goods. Blankets. That's it, Blaisdell. Tell him."

"You'll never get away," Blaisdell said after he finished shouting to Tyson.

Sundance didn't answer. Instead, he edged to the side of the door and called out, "You heard the boss man, Tyson! Get the guards down off the walls and do like he says. The guards with guns are to make a pile in the yard."

Tyson was a hard man and there was a long pause before he gave in. "You harm Mr. Blaisdell and you'll die slow."

"Send a man to get Myler and bring him here," Sundance ordered. "We're coming out now. Get the horses, Tyson."

The guards were in the yard when Sundance and the Actor came out with their guns pressed against Blaisdell's back. Shotguns and carbines clattered into a pile. Sundance looked up at the towers. The Gatlings still pointed at the yard; there was no one behind them. Prisoners who could watch from their cells begged Sundance to turn them loose, then cursed him when he wouldn't respond. He felt some pity for them, not much. A few might be innocent, or sentenced too harshly because they were poor, but he wasn't a judge and it wasn't his mission to right all the wrongs of the world.

A guard brought Myler, dazed and stumbling. Then there was the rattle of steel-shod hoofs, and Tyson came with the horses, the weapons, the supplies. Sundance unscrewed the top of a canteen and smelled the water.

"Drink some of it," he ordered Tyson. "Drink a lot."

Water ran down Tyson's chin as he drank. His heavy face was mottled with anger, but he remained silent. Then, prodding Tyson and Blaisdell in front of him, Sundance went to Bracken's cell and called out to him. "You took your God-damned time," Bracken roared.

He sounded drunk.

Tyson unlocked the door and Bracken came out waving a pistol. "Didn't know I had another one," he roared. "Did you, Indian? I'm taking over this jailbreak. You just follow orders. Now, *Mister* Blaisdell, I'm going to do a few things to you."

"Bracken!" Sundance's voice cracked like a whip. Bracken knew—suddenly he knew—and he tried to turn the gun. He nearly made it before Sundance shot him in the heart. He was dead before he hit the ground.

"That won't buy you anything," Blaisdell said. "One way or another, you're going to hang."

"Lock up the guards," Sundance said to Tyson. He nodded to Myler and the Actor. "The captain goes in last, after he opens the gates."

Now, a few minutes later, there was nothing to do but ride out. The Actor was no horseman, but he sat a saddle well enough. They went out through the gates followed by the furious howling of the remaining prisoners. Only Bracken had been killed.

He locked the gates and took the keys along. Down the hill, the cemetery was washed in the white glare of the lights. There were empty graves; Bracken would fill one of them.

Across the river the lights of the town winked in the darkness. The Actor was wearing one of Blaisdell's suits, far too big for him, and he grinned like a madman as he turned to look back at the Cage.

"I got out," he murmured. "Sundance, I'm free!"

They reached the road that went past the bottom of the hill. Myler coughed, swaying in the saddle. "You want to go with us, Actor?" Sundance asked. "You can if you like. It might not be so good for you alone."

"Do you need me?" the Actor said.

"We can manage," Sundance answered, wondering how the little man was going to fare in a world he hadn't seen for fifteen years.

"Then I'll say goodbye to you, my friend," the Actor said. "We'll never meet again, but you'll always have my thanks."

"My thanks to you, Mr. Maitland." They shook hands. "Get rid of the horse as soon as you can. It's got the jail brand on it. So long."

The prison fell away behind them, but the lights on the walls continued to glare for a long time. Then they faded and died. As they rode, Sundance kept waiting for the steam whistle to blow, but there was no sound except horse hoofs crunching in the gravel of the road. The sky was the dark blue of early evening and the wind was beginning to cool. Once they had to get off the road and wait behind a scatter of rocks while two men went by in a wagon. Sundance warned Blaisdell not to cry out, but he knew there was no need.

"How long are you going to hold me?" Blaisdell wanted to know.

"Long enough. You'll go back unharmed unless you try something."

"Would you have blown my arm off?"

"Sure I would," Sundance lied, knowing that compassion would be taken for weakness. "You run a rotten jail, Blaisdell. You should be hanged for the way you run that place."

"It works all right," Blaisdell said. "You'll be back there and you'll see how it works.

"Like hell," Sundance said, and that was no brag. He would die before he'd go back in the Cage. Mingo and his friends would be waiting.

Suddenly the steam whistle sounded from a long way

off. It wailed on the wind, thinned by distance but still clear enough to be heard for miles. Blaisdell smiled when he heard it. Myler did nothing but stare ahead, like a man trying to stay awake.

"I'm going to have to tie you," Sundance said. "We're not making good time and they'll be after us now—the tracker and the dogs."

There was no way to fool the dogs, not until they reached the desert. There the wild-blown sand, the ever shifting dunes, would blot out their scent. Sundance guessed Zorrilla would travel with another Mexican and send the dogs back with him once they lost the scent. Out there, the dogs would be useless, even a hindrance, so the tracker would send them back and continue the hunt on his own. Sundance wished he knew more about Zorrilla. How long would he keep up the chase? Some trackers were practical men, prepared to give up when pursuit brought no results. Others were absolutely unrelenting, ready to endure great hardships for the sake of the hunt. Zorrilla, Sundance figured, would belong to the second breed of men.

The White Sands desert lay directly to the east, beyond the last of thinly-settled country of ranchers and farmers. The desert was about a hundred miles long, and at least sixty miles wide, so there was no easy way to get around it. But the desert was to be their salvation or their damnation. It was a vast area of gypsum sand dunes and baking alkali flats. A handful of water holes dotted its surface, but they might be alkaline or dry. No towns existed there, for a town has to have a reason to exist, and in that desert there was none.

At midnight they rested the horses, watered them, fed them oats. They were sound animals, Sundance thought, but he longed to throw a saddle over Eagle, his great stallion. The horse he had would do all right for now.

Blaisdell refused to eat and Myler said he wasn't hungry. "Eat what I give you," Sundance told Myler. "Eat it and try to hold it down, then drink all the water you can hold. I told you not to die on me. I've gone to too much trouble."

"Nobody asked you," Myler said, hunched over a can of corned beef, sipping from his canteen.

Blaisdell wasn't too proud to refuse water. "Does that mean you deliberately got yourself sentenced to prison? My prison?"

"Myler was framed by the Indian Ring. If it had been any other jail besides yours I would have tried to get him out legally. But that would take time and Myler didn't have time. By the time I found the men who framed him, he would have been dead. That's the kind of jail you run, Blaisdell. Your flogging post and your Snake Hole."

Myler might not have been present, for all the notice Blaisdell took of him. "How do you know he was framed? I read his file so don't tell me he was framed. Three men swore that he murdered that man. Hold-out cards were found by the sheriff. What proof do you have that there was a conspiracy?"

Sundance turned to Myler. "Did you do it, Selden?"

Myler shook his head and resumed eating.

"That's all the proof I need," Sundance said. "Myler may be capable of murder—who isn't?—but he didn't kill the man in the poker game. As for cheating, I don't think he'd know how. It takes skill to cheat and Myler doesn't have it."

"That's why he got caught."

"Then why wasn't he caught before? He was Indian

agent at San Sebastian for fifteen years. How come nobody caught on to his cheating?"

"That's not the point. He was tried and sentenced. The law said he was guilty."

"The law says it's an innocent man's duty to escape, if he can. That's what Myler's doing, trying to stay alive long enough to establish his innocence. They can't send him back if he can do that."

Blaisdell took another drink of water. "They can *send you* back. There's no law to prevent that. You pleaded guilty to shooting that horse trader in Clovis. No matter what the reason was, you shot him and you got seven years for it."

Blaisdell was about to go on when Myler looked up angrily from his can of embalmed beef. "Why don't you shut up, turnkey, before I stuff a rock in your big mouth? You've been laying down that law to this man, and he's been listening to you, but I'll be damned to hell if I will. You lost your arm and you ran to that rat hole and hid for the rest of your life. Listen to me, head rat, I've seen men so wrecked and paralyzed they could move nothing but their eyes. So save your lousy law talk for somebody wants to listen to you!"

Blaisdell turned his head and stared out into the night.

"Easy, Selden," Sundance said, not wanting to lose his hostage to Myler's gun.

Myler glared at him. "Don't you start on me, either." Then he smiled a feeble smile. "What else have you got to eat? We're going to show this turnkey bastard what two decent men can do."

Chapter Ten

THEY rode on through the night, keeping to the road most of the time, leaving it only once when they got within half a mile of a trading post that Sundance had seen on his first journey east. Even so, a dog barked and they waited for the lights in the main house to go on. Nothing happened and they circled out wide until they got back on the road.

In places the road went across patches of soft sand; here it was paved with planks to keep wagons from sinking. Up ahead, there was a rickety bridge that spanned a muddy creek. This was the last flowing water they would see until they reached the far side of the desert.

They came to the first cache of supplies a few hours before first light. Everything was just as Sundance had left it weeks before. For now they were well supplied, but Sundance said, "We'll take everything. The next cache may be empty or torn up by animals."

"When are we going to rest?" Blaisdell asked. "You've been pushing us hard for over ten hours."

Myler gave a sneering laugh. "Will you listen to the turnkey!"

"Stop talking like a jailbird," Sundance said.

"Any jailbird is better than this rat," Myler said, scowling at Blaisdell.

The sun was up when Sundance finally called a halt at the place where the road gave out and became nothing but an old wagon track. A great split rock that looked like a church provided shade and a vantage point from which their back trail could be scouted with binoculars. "We'll sleep for two hours," Sundance said. "No more than that. We have to make the desert before Zorrilla catches up with the dogs. He may bring them part of the way in a light spring wagon. Get some sleep, Selden."

Myler crawled into the shadow of the rock and fell asleep as soon as he closed his eyes. Sundance put leg irons on Blaisdell; there was no way to handcuff a one-armed man. "Try anything and I'll pistol whip you," Sundance warned. "You're not strong enough or fast enough to take me. Believe that in advance and save yourself some pain."

Blaisdell glanced over at Myler. "When are you going to let me go?"

"I haven't decided yet. You're my ace, Blaisdell."

"Let me go and I'll call off the hunt."

"We don't know for sure they're coming this way. We were mounted when we left the jail. Dogs can't always track a man on horseback."

"Zorrilla will know even if the dogs don't. He'll be coming this way. Free me and I'll go back to meet him. I'll wait till he comes. Then I'll call it off. It's worth it to me. Zorrilla won't turn back unless I order him too."

"Why would you want to do that for me?"

"Not for you, for me. Take Myler and go far away from me. It'll be a blot on my record. One or two blots won't look so bad after fifteen years of service. This is a chance to get away."

"I have a chance to get away."

"You don't trust me."

"Not a bit. I wouldn't trust you even if I thought I could. Too much talk—sleep."

Sundance lay awake for a while, thinking about what lay ahead. If they got across the desert, they would have to skirt the Apache reservation that lay east of it. These Apaches were Mescaleros, fiercest of all the Indians, and even on the reservation they were a constant source of trouble. Small bands broke loose now and then; the reservation was so big that the agent and the Indian Police had trouble keeping track of them. They raided isolated ranches or went south to cross the border into Mexico, stealing horses there and taking them back, often with the connivance of the Indian Police who were expected to control them. To run into such a band meant trouble, for they were always on the lookout for horses and guns; they would kill for an old musket or a rusty knife. Just as bad were the Indians who served as bounty hunters. Never paid as much as the whites who hunted men for money, they were satisfied with what they got. There were no questions asked if they tortured the men they caught; to the Indians it meant being able to torture whites without being hanged for it.

If they rode far enough to the north, they might be able to avoid the Mescaleros. There was a tiny place called Oscura on the east side of the desert. After that there would be mountains and mountain forest, high hard country but better than the Apaches. For now they would follow the original plan, a more or less straight route across the desert, digging out the caches if they still existed. That done, Sundance would think about it again. Right now the big advantage was having horses, for no matter how swift a tracker was, he could hardly keep up with a horse. But it was possible that Zorrilla tracked from horseback; that could be done with well-trained dogs.

Sundance slept, and woke the others; they ate quickly before they went on. Even Blaisdell ate a can of beans, not that Sundance urged him, and then he waited with Myler while Sundance climbed up high on the rock and used the binoculars. There was nothing to see but dun hills and heat shimmer.

During the day he checked their back trail several times, but now there weren't so many high vantage points; the country was flat, broken only by stunted hills, as it sloped toward the desert. The desert was still many miles away, but it made its presence felt by the way it changed the light in the sky. Over the desert the light was whiter, harder, somehow hotter, than light elsewhere.

Sundance decided he would let Blaisdell go at the edge of the desert; give him a horse and supplies and point him back toward Sanderson. A hostage could be held just so long; after that, his value started to drop. Even now, someone who wanted Blaisdell's job might be directing the manhunt. When people had too long to consider the importance of a hostage, many times they concluded that he wasn't important enough. So it might be with Blaisdell, a man no one could like even with an effort. Besides, Sundance wanted to keep him alive, for what it was worth. Another hour and we'll be shot of him, he thought.

It was late in the afternoon when he heard the dogs baying from a long way back. If the wind hadn't shifted he wouldn't have heard them at all. But the deep-throated sound was unmistakable.

"Hear me out," Blaisdell said quickly.

Sundance drew the long-barreled Colt. "Mount up and ride. We're going to need you after all."

The dogs were coming fast and Sundance knew Zorrilla was tracking from the back of a horse. There was no other way he could have caught up to them so fast. In the near distance there was a dust cloud, a small one, which meant that Zorrilla wasn't riding at the head of a posse of jailkeepers and townspeople. Could even be that the Mexican was alone.

Soon they were in sight of the desert, red in the late afternoon sun. It seemed to stretch to infinity.

Myler said, "What do we do? Soon as we strike soft sand our pace has to slow."

"So does Zorrilla's," Sundance said. "We'll wait here and see if I can get a shot at him before we start across. A leg wound will take him out of the game. Watch Blaisdell. Watch him every minute and never mind what I'm shooting at."

Myler prodded Blaisdell behind a cluster of rocks and pointed a cocked pistol straight at his heart. Sundance climbed up and waited for the approach of the dogs and tracker. Using the binoculars, he looked back the way they had come. Then the dogs came yelping over a rise in the ground, four of them, wild with excitement. Sundance looked for Zorrilla and didn't see him.

He raised his head and a bullet spanged off a rock more than a foot away. Zorrilla can't be that bad a shot, Sundance thought. The rifle cracked again and the bullet struck the same place on the rock. No accident. The Mexican knew what he was doing.

The next time he looked, he was in a different place. Maybe the two well-placed shots were supposed to make him think Zorrilla didn't mean to kill him. The next well-placed shot could be right through the head—so he looked from a different place. Still no Zorrilla. He was aiming at one of the dogs when they ran down into a gully and disappeared. A silent whistle; it had to be that. The dogs stopped baying.

Zorrilla's voice came, high-pitched but loud enough to travel the distance. "Sundance, I could have killed you, the first shot. Let Mr. Blaisdell go. You do no good to keep him. Let him come out and we will make a deal. A bargain. Can you hear me?"

Sundance smiled. Mexicans were always offering deals. Usually a Mexican deal was the first step to killing a man. He guessed the Mexican was pretty close, not much more than a hundred and fifty yards, though sound carried a long way on the clear desert air.

Keeping his head down, he shouted back, "I'll make the deals. Go back—take the dogs—or I'll kill Blaisdell. You know he's still alive or the dogs would have found the body by now."

Zorrilla was shouting back when a rifle cracked, a long-range rifle by the sound of it. Sundance raised the binoculars and saw the Mexican sliding from the top of a chimney-like rock. The body continued to fall until it was caught in a cleft in the rock. It hung there, motionless. It was Zorrilla all right—the same red shirt, the same studded gunbelt he had seen in the prison yard.

"What was that shot?" Blaisdell wanted to know. His voice was tight, his face drawn with worry. No longer did he seem like a man with the power of life and death over others.

"Somebody killed Zorrilla," Sundance said, handing him the binoculars. "See for yourself. Watch your God-damned head or you'll lose it."

Blaisdell turned back to Sundance and his face was bewildered. "But my guards know Zorrilla. Everybody in Sanderson knows Zorrilla. Why would they shoot him?"

Sundance looked at the sky. "They didn't shoot him. I think we have some Indian Ring killers on our tail. A fast train with their horses on board. The telegraph brought them. It can't be anything else, Blaisdell. If they killed Zorrilla, then they mean to kill you too."

Blaisdell's face tightened, though not with fear. "Why kill me?"

"Why kill Zorrilla? Because they have orders to wipe the slate clean. Zorrilla led them to us, so they killed him."

Blaisdell wiped his face with his sleeve. "Why aren't they shooting?"

Rifle bullets answered his question. "They're shooting now," Sundance said. "We'll make a break for it as soon as the light gets bad. I'm going to give you a pistol—just remember they'll kill you just like the Mexican. No loose ends. If you're dead, who's to say I didn't do it?"

Sundance handed him the .44 Colt. "Don't point that thing at me," he said. "You won't make it."

Another scatter of bullets came at them like angry hornets. "Then Myler was telling the truth," Blaisdell said. He couldn't seem to take in what was happening.

"You're catching on," Sundance said.

Myler's anger boiled over. "Why don't you ask *me*, Blaisdell? Ask *me*—I'm not deaf. I told the truth and I got life. The law said 'life,' but you did your best to kill me. You and Tyson, you rat-faced son of a bitch!"

Myler was ready to go for the jailkeeper's throat. It wouldn't have been much of a contest: a sick man and a cripple. Sundance got between them just in time. "Ease off, Selden! The real enemy is out there. Five more minutes and we break out of here."

The sky was darker and approaching night thickened

the last of the light. "Time," Sundance said. "I'll cover you till you get clear. Forget about shooting back, you won't hit anything from a horse. Keep low and keep moving."

Three rifles cut loose as Myler and Blaisdell kicked their horses into a gallop and headed for the desert. There wasn't much to shoot at, but Sundance fired and kept on firing until the magazine was empty. Then he snatched up another rifle and sprayed the attacker's positions with bullets. Now all their fire was directed at him, and he rolled away and sprang into the saddle, digging with his heels, slapping the horse with his hat. A bullet nicked his shoulder; another lifted the hat from his head and sent it flying. Behind him he heard them yelling, but there was only sporadic firing after that. I've got to even the odds, he thought. It was three against three, but Myler and Blaisdell were no kind of army.

It was close to dark when he caught up to the others. Now there was a chance. Night, if you used it right, could be a very dependable ally. With night came cold and there was a pale moon that cast long shadows along the sides of the great rolling dunes. Later the moon would fade as the hours passed and then they could step up their pace.

"Stay in the shadows," Sundance warned. "A man and a horse make a good target against a patch of white sand. It will slow us up, but they won't find it easy to get us with a back-shot."

They were on foot, leading their horses. Blaisdell looked over his shoulder. "Why can't we stage an ambush?" he asked, his voice trailing away in indecision.

Sundance stared at him. Blaisdell had been away from the army too long. "Not yet," he said. "These men following us are no farmers rounded up for a posse. They've done this before—maybe not here, but they've done it. Our only chance is to put distance between us. Then we'll see about fighting back. Water may decide this. I have canteens buried at intervals."

Blaisdell frowned. "If they're still there, if you can find them."

Irritated, ready to flare up again, Myler said, "Nobody asked you to stick your nose in! If they're not there, maybe we'll die. There's a good chance of it. I wouldn't mind dying if you died first. On your rockpile, many's the time I asked for a swallow of water and didn't get it. What harm would it do to let a man have a mouthful of water, you mealymouth sneak?"

"Move on, Selden," Sundance said roughly. "You're talking too much and too loud. Blaisdell didn't put us here. Hate him if you like, but keep it in your head. Like it or not, we're in this together."

Myler made a spitting sound, one of his peculiarities. "We don't have to be," he said. "Blaisdell's no longer any good as a hostage. We can't use him to trade. All he's doing is drinking our water. I say let him make his own way."

Blaisdell turned to Sundance. "Is that what you want? I won't beg. Give me one canteen of water, let me keep the pistol I have. That's all I ask."

"I just told you men to move on," Sundance said. "Any more of this stupid bickering and I'll leave you both. You can shoot a gun, Blaisdell; that means you stay. Another reason I want you along, you're a witness to what's happening here."

"I'm a witness that you broke jail and killed a man."

Sundance remained patient. It was hard to be patient with both of them. "You can testify to that," he said.

"Just remember the rest of it, is all I want you to do."

"I'll say what I saw." Blaisdell made a purse mouth like a rich widow pursued by a too-ardent suitor.

Myler raged but kept it quiet. "For Christ's sake, Sundance, why do you take this kind of mush? You saved this bastard's life and all you get is— Here this hypocrite allows a swine like Bracken to ride roughshod over his stinking jail and he bleats about right and wrong! You saw the way Bracken lived, his carpet and his whiskey. His pervert boys and his pervert thugs dancing attendance, while all the time the rest of us were dying by inches."

Blaisdell bit his lip to keep from shouting. "It worked, you fool! A thing works or it doesn't. My prison worked. That's all I care about."

"Be seeing you, friends," Sundance said.

They remained silent after that. The moon grew pale and darkness came down on the desert. They won't be talking much when the sun comes up, Sundance thought. And when it comes up full force, they won't have enough energy to spit. Both men had spent a good part of their lives in the territory but had known no hardships. In their way, they had been petty rulers of their kingdoms, such as they were. But there the comparison ended; Myler was a decent man—Sundance didn't know what Blaisdell was. Certainly the jail-keeper's mind was twisted, fixed forever at the moment when he woke up in a military hospital and found that he was a cripple. They were alike in some ways, so different in others. But they were all he had.

It got bitter cold and Sundance told Myler to drape a blanket over his shoulders. What Myler needed was hot food and plenty of coffee. Instead of that, he ate cold beans and drank cold water when they rested the horses.

Sundance decided to push ahead for another two hours before he let them sleep. Had he been on his own, he would have traveled all night. No way to do that; by morning they would be falling over their feet.

He looked for a place with a clear field of fire and found it after they crossed a mile of dunes. The next stretch of desert was an alkali flat. Far out on the flat there was a clutter of rocks and cactus that could be defended; he told them that would have to do.

"An hour's sleep, no more than that," he said.

He didn't sleep himself but sat with his back to a rock, his eyes closed, all thought pushed from his mind, and in that way he rested. Not sleep, but close enough. He was aware of sounds and nothing else. If the killers came, he would hear them.

"I swear I just closed my eyes," Myler complained when he shook him awake.

"You slept like a stone," Sundance said. "How do you feel?"

"Don't keep asking me that like I'm a sick child." Myler rubbed his eyes and gave a jaw-cracking yawn. He took a drink of water. "Damn, that tastes like it's got ice in it."

"It would have if you left the cap off," Sundance said.

The sun boiled up in the sky and it was baking hot, though noon was many hours ahead. In the distance, beyond the plain, were more dunes, and they headed out, silent as men usually are in the morning. Behind them there was nothing, not a sign of life. Yet the desert was alive at that hour, before the brutal heat of the day set in. A horned toad ran over the rock and vanished; there were other creatures they couldn't see. Only man was the stranger here, Sundance thought. Wild things killed so they could remain alive; man killed for money, for all the unnatural reasons.

Scouting their back trail during the day, Sundance spotted their pursuers not once but twice. That didn't make sense, not much anyway, especially when the three men continued to hang back and keep following well out of rifle range.

"What do you think they're up to?" Myler asked. "Looks like they're not that eager to tangle with us."

Sundance looked at Myler, with his hollow chest and constant cough. After years of hiding in his office, Blaisdell wasn't in much better condition.

"Maybe not for the reasons you think," Sundance said. "I don't know what they're up to."

When night came, they made cold camp in a sandy hollow ringed with wind-polished rocks. It was cold and they huddled in their blankets. The horses were holding up all right, but water was running low. "How far is the next cache?" Myler said. "I would have thought you'd be more sparing with the water."

"It's better to carry it in your body than in a canteen," Sundance said. "People who don't believe that don't know the desert. That doesn't mean you should drink everything. Just drink a lot."

It was hard to sleep because of the biting cold; even with the blankets, they shivered. "Why haven't they done something?" Blaisdell said, staring out at the desert. "It's dark enough for an attack."

"We're not showing any lights," Sundance said. "You have to have something to shoot at when you attack a position."

Myler wasn't satisfied with that. "I don't like the way this is dragging on."

Sundance said, "If it drags on long enough, we'll be

clear of the desert. They can't know about the caches of water. Maybe they think they can just stroll in when we're half dead of thirst."

They stood guard in turns. Sundance wasn't sure that he could depend on Myler or Blaisdell to stand a good watch, but he knew he had to get some real sleep. A man who went too long without sleep couldn't trust what he saw, what he heard.

What woke him wasn't an attack but the howling of the wind. It wasn't anywhere close to gale force, yet the light was blotted out by blowing sand. Above the howl of the wind, he heard the terrified noises made by the horses. The wind grew stronger with every passing minute; they were right in the path of a sandstorm, a bad one by the sound of it. The horses were kicking and plunging, trying to break loose from the hobbles. Sundance pulled his bandanna up over his mouth and nose, feeling his eyes and ears filling with sand. The sandstorm swept over them with even greater fury and he saw the blurred shapes of Myler and Blaisdell stumbling in the darkness. "Use your blankets to cover your heads," he shouted. "Get down behind the rocks and hang on!" Then, wrapping his own head, he tried to get to the horses, but the wind knocked him down and rolled him several times until he was stopped by a rock. Struggling up, he heard the horses tearing loose, galloping madly as though carried on the wind. There was nothing he could do to stop them; if the storm didn't let up, they would die.

Covered or not, he was breathing in fine sand, gagging as it dried the moisture in his throat. Now the storm was at its worst, blotting out earth and sky, doing its best to kill him. The wind howled on and on, and when he tried to move, he felt the weight of sand pressing against him. He tried to call out to the others, but nothing came out but a rasping sound without shape or meaning. And then, as quickly as it had come, the storm began to ebb. The wind dropped from a howl to a wail, and then it faded and died.

There was no light when he looked up at the sky. Finally, he was able to see his hand, and after that the figures of Myler and Blaisdell buried in sand. Coughing and spitting, he crawled over to where they were and dug the sand away with his fingers. He caught the end of Myler's blanket and jerked it free. Then he shook Myler and ended by slapping him. Myler tried to vomit but nothing came up.

"Look for the canteens," Sundance shouted. "I've got to dig out Blaisdell."

Myler spat sand. "I heard the horses going away."

Sundance prodded him into action. "The hell with the horses—find the water!"

Blaisdell was unconscious when he dug him out, his mouth so filled with sand that Sundance had to use his fingers to get it out. He put his ear to Blaisdell's chest. There was a heartbeat, but it was light and rapid. Quickly, he lifted Blaisdell until he was hanging face down over a rock and struck him repeatedly in the small of the back. At last, with a great, convulsive gasp, Blaisdell began to breathe.

"I found one canteen," Myler shouted.

"Get it over here. Blaisdell is in a bad way."

Sundance spilled water into Blaisdell's mouth and shook him awake. "Drink more," he ordered, and when Blaisdell was finished, still gasping, he handed the canteen to Myler.

The sky was beginning to clear by the time they were able to talk without sucking in air. Sundance gave

Blaisdell more water before he drank himself.

Oddly, Myler was in a jubilant mood. "I thought we were dead men," he said, slapping sand from his clothes. He pulled off his boots and emptied them of sand. "I thought that wind was about to tear off my head! If I live to be a thousand, I hope to never go through that again."

At last, the moon could be seen through the high-blown sand that still drifted across its face. The shape of their camping place had changed. Myler pointed. "There were rocks there. Now they're gone. It's like everything has been turned around."

"What are we going to do?" Blaisdell said at last. His face, always pale, was the color of marble in the moonlight. "After that storm, do you think we'll find the next cache of water?"

"I don't know," Sundance said. "That's something to think about later. We still have water in the canteens if we can find them. Right now all we can do is dig."

Chapter Eleven

IT was morning before they found the canteens and the other supplies. The wind had dragged or thrown them in all directions. Using the binoculars, Sundance saw the shapes of the dead horses a long way behind the camp. He counted them; one was missing, but that just meant that one horse was buried deeper than the others.

"No more horses," he said, shifting the glasses when he spotted what looked like a body half covered with sand. "And maybe no more men following us."

Followed by Myler and Blaisdell, he walked out from the camp holding the Winchester at the ready. They found the dead man and after they dug out the body, they found a rifle still clutched in his hand. After a lot of searching they found the others, knocked down by the storm and suffocated. Rifles were with the bodies.

"They got caught in the open when the storm hit," Sundance said. "No blankets, no cover—they just filled up with sand and died."

"They were coming to attack us," Myler said. "It has to be that."

"Maybe so," Sundance said. "Or coming in close to see what we were doing. They might have been trying to run off the horses. Their own horses must be as dead as ours. We could search for their water, but I'd say we best go on with what we have."

"Why not take the time to find their water?" Myler said. "They're dead."

Sundance said, "They're not the only ones looking for us. There could be a posse not too far back. I figure we've come more than half way across this desert. Time to go the rest of the way."

They ate, then cleaned their guns before they started out again. The storm might never have happened; the sky was a hard, bright blue without a cloud or a trace of blowing sand.

"About twenty more miles," Sundance said after they had spent two hours searching for the last cache of water without success. The storm had buried the landmark where the water should have been. That was the chance you took when you hid things in the desert. "That's not so bad. We'll take it slow. When we get out we'll head for Dobson Getty's, where my horse is."

Blaisdell said, narrow-eyed, "That's the man you shot."

Sundance smiled. "This time I think he'll sell me the horse. Last time was a misunderstanding."

"I don't believe any of this," Blaisdell said. "You worked the whole thing with Getty."

"Getty won't tell you that. Neither will I. Sorry to disappoint you, Blaisdell, but nobody's going to your jail. Forget you're a jailkeeper for a while. We're not out of this yet."

"But those killers are dead."

"The Indian Ring has plenty of killers. All they have to do is riffle through a stack of money and the killers come a-running."

A long day's walk took them about fifteen miles to the edge of the desert. By then, Blaisdell and Myler were staggering, and they fell down like walking wounded when Sundance called a halt for the night.

Here, in the lee of a stony rise, there was brush, and they were able to make a small fire. They heated corned beef and crunched on hard biscuits while the coffee boiled. Myler dipped his biscuits in the coffee because he said they were threatening to break his teeth. "Funny how the worst food tastes better when it's hot," he said. "All except what you get in the Cage, that is. I was thinking that maybe I don't want to go back for a new trial."

"Then why are we here?" Sundance asked. "You're going back, Selden. The world needs upright citizens like you."

"Didn't look like it did. The last few nights I was able to sleep without dreaming I was back in the Cage with the walls of the cell closing in on me. That was because I figured I wouldn't be going back. I don't want to start sweating in my sleep again, Sundance."

Sundance didn't tell Myler that the nightmares about the Cage would come back. There was no way to shake off an experience like that. Years from now, if Myler lived that long, there would be nights when the bad dreams would come swimming up out of the dark parts of his brain. Dreams like that came at the most unexpected times. A man might go to bed with nothing bothering him, and then, somewhere in the night, he would wake up screaming. As time passed, you got so you could handle the nightmares; just the same, they never went away.

Myler said, "If I go back there's no telling what might happen, and that's a chance I don't have to take. You might say my faith in the law has been shaken. Not shaken—all shot to hell! All through my trial I kept thinking something would save me even while my life and liberty were being perjured away by three strangers."

"I never knew you to talk so much," Sundance said.

"Maybe I never talked enough," Myler said. "You came to the Cage to get me out. You did. I can't repay you for that."

"You can repay me by going back with Blaisdell."

"Where's the evidence that will clear me, Sundance? Blaisdell's no friend of mine. Hardly that. Blaisdell is the friend of no man."

Drinking coffee, the jailkeeper remained silent.

Sundance said, "You'll be a wanted man for the rest of your life, if you don't go back. You're not cut out for the outlaw life, Selden. Your posters will be up all over the place. Think of that."

Blaisdell said, "He can't. He's asleep. I have to ask you something. Something that will help to clear my own thoughts."

"What is it?"

"When the prison gates closed behind you and you saw how bad it was, did you curse yourself for a fool and want to take it all back?"

"A little," Sundance said. "But you can't go back on what you've done. The urge is there but you can't do it. You face that because there's nothing else to do. You learn to work in the here and now, Blaisdell."

Blaisdell rolled himself in his blanket and turned over on his side. "I wish I'd learned to do that," he said.

Another day took them out of the desert. The water was gone and there was none in sight. Early the next morning they found a waterhole and drank the foul tasting water without thinking about it. When they finished, there was enough water left to fill one canteen.

"We should hit Oscura sometime tomorrow," Sundance said.

"What about the law?" Myler said.

"No law," Sundance said. "Just a few houses, a handful of Mexicans. Harmless people with no love for law of any kind."

"Smart Mexicans," Myler said.

"We can get water there, buy food, maybe horses. If not horses, mules. After that, we'll head for Getty's place. There are mountains to cross, but there's a good clear trail. Just as long as we have water and food."

They came to Oscura and the villagers, alarmed by their appearance, vanished as soon as they saw them coming. Dirty, caked with sand and salt, they stood in the center of the town, while Sundance called out in Spanish, explaining that they meant no harm to anyone.

"We have money," he shouted. "I will throw money on the ground so you will see we can pay for what we want."

The sound of money striking a rocky place brought the Mexicans from their hiding places. An old man, the village leader, emerged with his straw sombrero in his hands. He looked at the money, but made no attempt to pick it up. Sundance showed him paper money and he bowed, saying, "We are honored, señor."

They crossed the mountains on muleback; a fourth mule packed the supplies. In the high country, on a slope dotted with pines, Sundance shot a deer and they ate well for the first time since leaving the Cage, and there was coffee and canned peaches to go with the deer meat. Sitting by the fire, Sundance felt a sort of peace. It might not last very long, but he had learned to take life one hour at a time.

It took them four days to cross the mountains, and at no time was there any sign of pursuit. Myler began to fill out, eating more than he had to, and then eating some more. Blaisdell didn't seem to bother him so much now, though he did make occasional remarks, but more from habit than anything else. Blaisdell remained silent for the most part, doing what he was told, making no trouble. Even so, Sundance watched him all the time, especially when night came.

On the last night in the mountains, they traveled on long after it was dark, made camp in a hollow that protected them from the wind, and when they woke up the next morning they saw the flatlands stretching out before them. Myler said what Sundance was thinking: "Down there is nothing but trouble. I could stay in these mountains for the rest of my life. We could do that, Sundance."

"Wouldn't be practical, Selden. Somebody would find us sooner or later. It wouldn't have to be the law. Some prospector. Some army surveying expedition. Word would get out and the law would climb up after us."

Myler glared at him. "I wish you could be a bit more reckless," he said.

"You're turning wild, Selden. Anybody looking at you would take you for a hardened criminal!"

They rode northeast, keeping well away from the boundary of the Mescalero reservation, traveling by night, sleeping by day. No Apaches showed themselves; no Apache was seen who didn't want to be seen. They might be anywhere, Sundance thought. So they stood watches even during the day; at night, Sundance rode ahead to check for places where they might be ambushed.

Myler didn't like the idea that they might be attacked by runaways from the reservation. "Treat the Indians right and you don't have to be afraid of them," he declared pompously. "An Indian is just like any other man. You have to be kind, but you have to be firm too. Let the Indian know who's boss and he respects you for it. You may be half Indian, Sundance, but I think I know more about Indians than you do."

"Sure you do," Sundance agreed, thinking what a horse's ass Myler was.

"The Indians are children and you have to treat them like children," Myler went on. "Well, not exactly as children. What I mean is, they have to be cared for, protected from the things that threaten to destroy them. Civilization's all right in its way, but too much of it can be fatal. What's best for the Indian, in my opinion, is to keep his life simple. I don't know that he'll ever learn to be an efficient farmer or stockman. I've made some efforts in that direction, and I'm sorry to say that nothing worked out too well. However, when I get back to San Sebastian . . ."

Sundance smiled. "I thought you were set on becoming an outlaw?"

Myler got angry, an easy thing for him. "I leave that open for the moment," he said.

"How much farther to Getty's place?" Myler asked after they had gone another day. Blaisdell was riding ahead of them, lost in his own thoughts, which appeared to be gloomy. Men who led tidy lives sometimes were badly confused when the world crowded in on them.

"Two more days," Sundance said. "We'll have to scout the town before we go in. We don't know what's waiting there."

"Meaning you don't trust Getty?"

"No more than I have to. The old man is reliable if he knows it's dangerous not to be. All I want from Getty is my horse, and then we'll be gone."

"Then why not leave the horse? We have horses."

"Not horses like that horse, Selden."

"A horse is just another animal," Myler said, the well-intentioned crank so sure of what was right for everyone. "Seems to me you're taking us out of our way just for a whim."

"Give your mouth a rest," Sundance said. "It's hard to watch for trouble, with you talking all the time. We're going for my horse and that's the end of it."

Myler didn't understand the bond that could exist between man and animal. There could be affection without sentimentality. The Indians, least maudlin of all people, knew that without having to put it into words. White men used so many words that could be left unsaid.

Sundance guessed they were clear of the Mescaleros by now. In the dime novels, the Indians always used smoke signals to warn of the approach of strangers. The world outside books was different, as most things were; real Indians just watched and waited, taking no chances, for they seldom had the numbers, the firepower. It wasn't going so bad, he thought. They had survived the desert and the men who tried to creep up on them in the storm. They had food and water and weapons; a good chance of making it across the Texas line. The hunt wouldn't stop there—federal marshals would dog them, but Texas had plenty of badmen and the whole country wouldn't be looking for two escaped convicts from New Mexico.

This was dry country but it wasn't desert and the going was easy enough if they didn't push it too hard. They came to an old wagon road with weeds growing in the ruts.

"This will take us to Getty's village," Sundance said. "Just keep a sharp lookout from here on. Most of the Mexicans work for Getty or owe him money, but they may decide to go into business for themselves. One more day will take us there. We make camp for the night, then go in just after first light. Getty keeps them happy with beer and maybe they'll be sleeping it off."

They made better time by keeping to the road; at the end of the day they had traveled nearly thirty miles. Sundance pointed to a chain of low hills in the distance. "Beyond there," he said. "Tomorrow night we'll check our weapons just in case the Mexicans get frisky. They're dirt poor and Getty takes all the money they have. Reward money always looks good to a poor man."

"It might look good to old Getty," Myler said.

"It might," Sundance agreed. "I don't think so, but it might."

"Don't you trust anyone?" Blaisdell asked.

Thinking of Crook, Sundance said, "A few people, Blaisdell. No more than that, and that's enough."

They reached the hills before sundown and crossed them in the dark, then slept for four hours. Before they left, they cleaned their weapons and loaded them, making sure there was extra ammunition close to hand. If the Mexicans attacked, they would try to fight them off. Getty had a lot of Mexicans, but Sundance thought they could do it. The hard part would come if the Mexicans followed them all the way to the Texas line, sniping at them by night, trying to run off their horses.

The sun was coming up when they caught sight of the village. Dogs barked, but dogs barked all night in Mexican villages. No smoke from cook fires came from the straggle of houses. They topped a hill, dismounted and left their horses out of sight. Lying on his belly, Sundance moved the binoculars from one end of town to the other, and he felt a surge of excitement when he spotted Eagle moving in the corral to one side of Getty's saloon. The big stallion looked to be in fine shape, moving restlessly inside the stout rails of the corral. As if sensing Sundance's presence, the stallion raised his head, pawing at the gate.

"We'll give it a few more minutes," Sundance said. Again, he scouted the village with the binoculars, moving the twin lenses to places where men might hide. Nothing moved, and even the dogs were quiet for a while.

"Keep your shotguns ready," Sundance warned as they started down from the hill. "But don't fire till I tell you. You fire first, and we'll catch lead, no matter how friendly they are."

They rode their horses at a walk, moving closer to the town. Eagle whinnied. Sundance rode up to the corral and said, "Easy, boy. You'll be out of there in a minute. Quiet, boy."

Weapons cocked and ready to fire, they moved down the street, and were nearly at the end of it when an old man came out of a house, unbuttoning his pants. His eyes widened in terror when he saw their faces, their guns; in a moment he would run or yell.

Sundance smiled at him, saying in Spanish, "We are not here to rob or to kill. No noise, you understand. Is Getty in his house?"

The old man's head bobbed on his neck. "Yes, he is

asleep. All are asleep but me. You do not want to shoot me?"

"Nobody's going to shoot you, grandfather," Sundance said. "Walk along with us to Getty's house and it will be all right. Then you will tell Getty to come out so we will know that he is not hiding somewhere else. As a favor to us, you will do that."

The saloon door was closed and barred from the inside; the old man bowed to Sundance and knocked on it. "Señor Getty," he called. "It is Francisco and I would talk with you. Open up, Señor Getty."

The old man had to knock three times before Getty's grumbling voice answered. "Get away from here, *borracho!* Not open for business for another hour. Drunkard, you can drink then."

Sundance banged on the door. "Open up, Dob. It's Sundance. Open up or I'll break it down. Wake up, Dob. It's Sundance!"

"He was drunk last night," the Mexican explained apologetically. "So was I."

The door banged open and Getty, blinking with gummy eyes, looked at them over the barrel of a rifle. "God Almighty," he said, lowering the muzzle. "It *is* you. I thought I was dreaming for a minute. For days I been expecting you to show up."

Getty opened the door all the way and told them to come in. "I got to drink a beer to get my eyes open. If I didn't see it, I wouldn't believe it. How are you and what are you doing out of jail?"

Chapter Twelve

SUNDANCE drew his gun and pointed it at Getty. "Never mind how I am, old man. What I'm doing out of jail is I broke out of jail. You're the reason I was in there, you thief! Say hello to Superintendent Blaisdell, head jailer of the Sanderson Penitentiary. He's the reason I got out."

Getty looked at Myler. "Who's he, the assistant superintendent?"

"You don't have to go through with this charade," Blaisdell said.

Getty got back to Sundance. "What's that word mean—charade?"

"Superintendent Blaisdell thinks we're play-acting. He thinks you had something to do with getting me into his jail. Tell him how wrong he is. Tell him so he won't think you're a man doesn't have respect for the laws of New Mexico."

The old man assumed a pious air as he spoke to Blaisdell. "I am right sorry to find you in the clutches of this vicious criminal, sir. No man in shoe leather has more respect for the law than yours truly, Dobson Getty. This renegade James Sundance attempted to take from me what was rightfully mine. Shot me when I said he could not have it. I thought I had seen the last of this

167

scoundrel, Mr. Blaisdell. Now, sir, I am shocked to find him on the loose. Meaning no offense, sir, how is it that I find this villain pointing a loaded revolver at me? I am a citizen and a taxpayer, and I intend to protest to the highest authority."

"You can stop now," Sundance said. "Superintendent Blaisdell gets the idea. This other man is Selden Myler, the celebrated murderer."

"Please to meet you," Getty said.

"Stop it," Blaisdell said. "There's no need for any of this. I know what happened. I know you were part of it, Mr. Getty, but that doesn't matter to me. Not any more."

"That's your opinion, sir," Getty said. "I admit only to my good name. Would you care for a drink? My saloon is open for business and I am at your service. What about you, Mr. Myler? I'm afraid I can't serve you, Mr. Sundance. Selling liquor to Indians is against the law. Threaten me all you like. You can't have as much as a glass of beer. Stick to black coffee, sir. You won't get in trouble if you stick to that."

Getty set up beer for Blaisdell, whiskey for Myler, coffee for Sundance. Then he went to fry up a big batch of steak and onions and country potatoes.

Sundance asked, "Anybody been looking for us?"

Getty knocked back a drink. "Even asked for you by name, these three fellas did. Would that be of interest to you?"

Sundance said it would. "When did they ask?"

"A few days back," Getty said. "Lawmen they said they were, though there was no tin in sight." Getty looked at Blaisdell. "Tin, sir, is the name criminals give the badges carried by our peace officers. No badges were displayed and none asked for by me."

Sundance said, "Hurry it up, Dob. What happened?"

"Not a thing," Getty said. "These three men were spotted by my Mexicans long before they arrived here. My Mexicans were alarmed by the sight of these three strangers—we get so few visitors here—and having informed me, my Mexicans took cover and waited. The three men rode in and said they were looking for three convicts from the Cage. Said they were holding the superintendent hostage. Even for lawmen, they were very tough about how they asked their questions. They wanted to know if I still had your horse. I said yes, and then they asked to see the horse. To make sure I still had it and you hadn't come along to take it away."

"Did they get to see my horse?" Sundance asked.

"No," Getty said. "They were so loud that my Mexicans appeared. About ten or twelve Mexicans, all wanting to know what was wrong. At which time the three men said nothing was wrong and they must have been given wrong information, and we parted the best of friends, and my Mexicans escorted them out of town to make sure nothing happened to them. I'm a man believes in doing things right, so some of my Mexicans escorted them all of fifty miles from here. Funny thing. One of them, a big moose of a man, has a habit no man I've seen lately has—chewing cloves."

Myler looked up quickly. "Did you say cloves?"

"It's no worse than dipping snuff," Getty said.

"A big man that sweated a lot?"

"You know him, Selden?" Sundance said.

"Ringelman, one of the men who framed me. What were the others like, Mr. Getty? Was one short and dark and fidgety? The other with a bulb nose and big ears? Near as big as the one who chewed cloves?"

"Haggard is the short one," Myler said. "Woodruff is the other. It has to be them."

"They described the three convicts?" Sundance asked Getty.

"They described you and Mr. Myler better than the third man," Getty said. "It did seem to me they described Mr. Myler better than anybody. Like they knew him real well."

Myler gave the table a whack. "Why wouldn't they? They spent a whole evening playing cards with me. I'll bet they're hiding out there, waiting for us to come along."

Getty said, "Not close to here. I told you my Mexicans saw them fifty miles off my property. If they try to come back, they'll be spotted. They rode east. They may figure you're headed for the Texas line. I'd say they can be found over in that country. Funny thing. They don't have the look of real gunmen, except maybe the one you call Haggard. He's a shifty little bastard, like you say. But they don't have the mark of true killers. You get to know when men are happy in their work. These boys looked kind of mournful."

"They're following orders they don't like?" Blaisdell said, looking at Sundance. "Why don't they just take off? There's a lot of country to hide in between here and Canada."

Sundance said, "I'm only guessing they have families, land they want to hang on to. They got into something that looked easy at the time. Help frame a man into jail for life, take the money, forget about the whole thing. Now he's back from the dead and they have to get rid of him for good. The Indian Ring agents have ordered them to kill Myler and me while we're still fugitives. I don't know why they haven't been killed by the Ring, to shut them up for keeps. That may happen yet. For now, they're under orders to get us."

"Then why doesn't Myler go back with me, right now?" Blaisdell said. "I'll tell what I've seen. Mr. Getty will verify the fact that these men came looking for you and Myler."

"What could you say, Blaisdell? That three men followed us in the desert and got killed by a sandstorm? When a convict breaks out, he's fair game for any man, as you know all too well. Haggard, Woodruff and Ringelman have every right to hunt us, kill us, do anything to put us out of the way. If the law even bothered to ask them questions, they could say they were in fear of their lives. Why wouldn't they try to kill us to protect their own lives?"

"What about the killing of Zorrilla?"

"No good, Blaisdell. Nobody knows for sure who killed him. One of the three men, sure. They're all nothing but bones by now, and even the bones are scattered and buried in the sand."

Sundance got up from the table. "What's a good guess where they're holed up, Dob?"

Getty scratched his strange-looking hair. "Not any of the big towns along the Texas line, that's for sure. They're not professional manhunters, but they know they won't find you there. The law can't watch every foot of the line, so they'll go where they think you'll show up sooner or later. Some small place, small as where you are now. Or they may just ride the Texas line and hope to get lucky. You ask too-hard questions, Sundance. I don't know what they'll do. Good advice is to slip across into Texas and get the hell away from New Mexico."

"We have to find them," Sundance said. "It's no

good if we don't. How about we borrow some of your Mexicans? They'll be paid and so will you."

The old man looked alarmed. "Hold on there, sonny! Here is home and here I stay. Don't try to get me mixed up in this."

"Nobody said you had to go, Dob. What about the Mexicans?"

Getty said no. "You're better off without them. Probably I could keep them in line, not you. You don't want to get back-shot for the jail rewards, do you? I have to confess my Mexicans are like to do that if they get the chance. They are not the most dependable of God's creatures, not by a long shot. I'm just looking out for your best interests, Sundance."

"Sure, Dob. We'll be going now. I hope you've been telling the truth and nothing but the truth, so help you God."

The old man raised his right hand. "On a stack of Bibles." He turned to Blaisdell. "These men are innocent, sir. Of that you can be sure. Me, I'm twice as innocent."

They were riding out when Blaisdell said, "I wouldn't trust Getty as far as I could throw him. You don't either, yet you don't want to see him in jail."

"I wouldn't mind seeing him in jail. I just don't want to be the one that puts him there. There's a difference, Blaisdell. You make a deal—a real deal—you keep it. Otherwise your word is no good, and that gets around after a while. Can you understand that?"

"I'm beginning to," Blaisdell said. "It's taken me a good many years. You've never had any doubts, have you? You decide what you're going to do, and you do it. I don't mean to be sarcastic. I just wonder what it must be like to be a man like you."

"You're doing it late in life, Blaisdell. You ran that prison. It didn't run by itself."

"But how was I to distinguish one man from another? The men I got weren't sent to me for nothing. Murderers. Maniacs. Human savages. The worst people in the world. My job was to keep them locked up, and that's what I did. Brutal men have to be treated brutally. There wasn't an instant when I didn't feel my life was in danger."

"You face danger just by waking up in the morning. There's nothing more to be said. I have no answers for you. A long time ago you decided what your life was going to be like."

"It was decided for me," Blaisdell said. "There was nothing else for me to do."

"You could have run a store, clerked in an office, taught school. But you wanted to prove how hard you were, and the Cage gave you the chance. Now you're having second thoughts about your life. I don't like you, Blaisdell, and nothing you say can change that. Myler needs your help, but I don't. So do the poor bastards back in your stinking jail. That's what you should be thinking about."

"Perhaps I am," Blaisdell said.

That night they saw the light of a campfire, a big one, and even at the distance of a mile they heard singing and yelling. Myler looked apprehensive, and Sundance said, "Saddle tramps, that's all. No posse would be making that kind of noise."

Even so, they stood guard. Even a posse might decide to get drunk, but nothing happened by the time dawn came. In the morning Sundance saw a small party of Mexicans and recognized one of them as a Getty man. It was the sheepherder or goatherder who didn't want to pay interest on his liquor bill.

"They're over there on a knob watching the road," Sundance said, coming back into camp. "I guess they're all right, but we'll back-track and go around them."

They had to go a long way back before it was safe to ride out wide without being spotted. After that, they saw no one else for the rest of the day. That night, Myler grumbled because Sundance said they were going to make cold camp—no fire, no hot food—but Blaisdell was uncomplaining and ate what there was to eat: salt pork and beans.

"Some day they're going to learn how to keep things from spoiling without salt," Myler said.

Sundance smiled, amused by Myler's perpetual crankiness. The man had more ideas for changing the world than the most strident lady reformer from New England. Since their long journey began, Myler had discoursed on any number of subjects: the unpredictability of the Colorado River, which was always flooding half the country when it ran wild, the use of large dogs as beasts of burden, the evils of Dr. Pedro's Famous Elixir For Nervous Ladies.

"No wonder they aren't nervous after they drink some of that," Myler declared. "It's two parts alcohol and one part opium."

"Maybe they should give some Dr. Pedro to the Colorado River," Sundance said. "While they're at it, they should give some to you. Why can't you settle down and enjoy the scenery? Travelers come from all over the world to marvel at the scenery of New Mexico. Used to bring sketchbooks, now they fetch along cameras."

Looking up from the slab of streaky pork, Myler said, "I must say you're in a good mood today. Not like you at all, the way I remember you."

Sundance ate his beans and was glad to have them. "You haven't changed at all, Selden. If it's raining you say you're going to catch a cold. If it's hot and dry, you're afraid of coming down with fever. Sure I'm in a good mood. I'm out of Blaisdell's jail, the sun is shining, I have food, my horse back, and—don't you forget it—I'm free!"

Myler sulked over his salt meat, but at last he said, "You're right. I'm free too. Why do you suppose I keep forgetting that?"

"Because you don't want to remember when you weren't free," Sundance said quietly. "Loosen your stays, Selden, and enjoy what you have."

"Here today and gone tomorrow, is that it?"

"It's not gone yet, you damned crank! Now, you were saying about keeping things from spoiling without using salt. They call that 'refrigeration,' Selden. You've been buried down in San Sebastian so long you haven't keep up with what's going on in the world. Ice-cold cars, that's how they get the meat east from the Chicago packing plants. Don't ask me how they do that, Selden. I was hoping you could tell us."

"I can tell you what you can do in your hat," Myler snorted.

"People have told me that," Sundance admitted. "What I'm interested in is these large dogs of yours. You say the Dutch have tried it. How did they make out?"

Myler's answer came out in a grudging manner. "You're just trying to make a fool of me, but I'll tell you so you won't be as ignorant as you are. The Dutch are very thrifty people—the Holland Dutch, I mean—and they decided why shouldn't big dogs pay their way like the other big critters, horses, mules, donkeys, camels, elephants. So they hitched these big dogs to milk carts and so forth, and that worked pretty well, and pleased with that, they said why shouldn't cats pull their freight."

Sundance wished he had some coffee to warm up the cold bacon and beans in his belly. "Must have been a lot of spilled milk in Holland."

Myler snorted his annoyance. "There was, as it turns out. The damn fool Dutch didn't realize any animal has to be trained before you make it work."

"You ever try to train a cat, Selden?"

"The hell with you, Sundance! You asked me and I'm answering and you're acting like a jackass, which you are. The world's never going to make any progress as long as mockers like you are around."

Blaisdell stayed awake long after Myler pulled his blanket over his head and went to sleep. "He's a crank but he's a good man," he said. "Is there any reason why you keep putting the knife into him?"

"A very small knife, Blaisdell. I know he's a good man, but when a man thinks he's better than other men, there's nothing to do but make a small cut to let the gas out. It won't do any good."

"Then why do it?"

"Because he gets under my skin. You think I shouldn't be that human?"

"I suppose not," Blaisdell said, and he walked away and sat on a boulder without moving. Sundance looked at his back, sensing the man's misery, but there was no solace he could offer, or wanted to offer. All lives were separate, when all was said and done, and, he thought, we all go to our separate graves, even if we are buried in a pit during a cholera epidemic. Once again, thinking of the Cage, he felt a twitch of dislike for Blaisdell. Oh, what the hell—I just want to get this over with and be gone from Myler and Blaisdell, he thought.

Blaisdell came back to camp. "There's a light out there," he said. "It was there and now it's gone. It winked on and off."

Blaisdell went up before Sundance and pointed. "Where?"

"Out there," he said. "It was like the flare of a match and then it went out."

Sundance looked and saw nothing but the night. It could be something, it could be nothing. In the dark, tired eyes produced lights, flashes, that meant nothing. But Blaisdell might be right. He was a cold man and he hadn't panicked yet, not during the jailbreak, not in the desert—he had no feelings, or he had lost what he had.

Now he was annoyed because Sundance wouldn't confirm what wasn't there any longer. "I saw it—out there."

"Stop pointing in all directions, Blaisdell. Where did you see the light?"

"Dead east."

The light flared again. "A match," Sundance said. "Somebody lighting a lamp by a window. There it goes."

It was lamplight sure enough; it remained steady after the match went out. It was too dark to see anything else. "It's miles away," Sundance said. "If it burns all night, it could mean we're supposed to see it."

"People do leave lights on all night," Blaisdell said.

"Not in this country where oil is so hard to come by," Sundance said. "Wake up Myler and we'll take a look from a long way off."

They got off the road after they had gone a mile.

There was no moon and the going was slow because they had to cross a long stretch of ground covered with rocks that would break a horse's leg like a stick, and it was well over an hour before they got to the other side of it. Finally, a watery moon broke through the clouds and they were able to see the dark outlines of buildings in the distance. Far behind the town were ragged hills—the Texas line.

"A town with just one light in it," Sundance whispered. "Must be abandoned. We'll wait here till morning, then I'll use the glasses to see what it is. Watch the horses so they don't get loose. No talking, no noise of any kind. It may be some desert rat or scavenger prowling about. But we're not going there in the dark."

No one slept after that. They hobbled the horses, all but Eagle; the well-trained stallion would move only when ordered by Sundance. The horses were skittish, but they settled down to graze on tufts of dry, yellow grass. The light remained bright and steady as the night passed; it still burned as red streaked across the morning sky.

It was a ghost town, so called; a single street of ramshackle buildings in the middle of nowhere, one of a hundred such towns in all parts of the West. There was an ore dump about a mile from the south end of town and rusting machinery was reddened by the rising sun. The light still burned in the window, though it was hard to see it because of the sun. No signs of men or animals; no smoke came from the house where the light was.

"They're nowhere near that light," Sundance said. "That's why it's still burning. I'm guessing they'll turn up after a while."

They waited and it was hot lying in the brush with the wind blowing dust in their faces. The town baked in utter silence, a dead place that had known noisy Saturday nights, the shrill laughter of whores fighting to separate miners from their money. Sooner or later, the place would burn down, fired by a lightning bolt or a cigarette stub dropped by some wanderer.

"What are we going to do?" Myler whispered.

"Nothing right now."

Blaisdell was using the binoculars. "There's something stirring at the top of that ore dump. Rocks falling like somebody's going down the back of it."

Sundance took the glasses and trained them on the dump. As he moved the glasses, a man came round the side of the dump, holding a rifle and shading his eyes against the sun. The glasses were powerful and Sundance was able to bring him close. A big man in a sweated shirt, chewing and spitting as he moved.

"Take a look," Sundance said to Myler. "Is that Ringelman?"

"It's him." Myler was quivering with excitement. "Shoot the bastard!" His voice got loud and Sundance clapped his hand over Myler's mouth. Myler struggled until Sundance shook him into silence.

"One shot and the others will dig in deep," Sundance whispered. He took the glasses and watched Ringelman as he made his way through the thick brush to the end of the street. Then he saw him wave to a man who dropped down from a roof; in an instant they were gone from sight.

"Why are you letting them get away like that?" Myler whispered, sullen and angry.

"I could miss at this range," Sundance said. "I can only shoot one man at a time. You think you can do better?"

"Now we'll be stuck out here all day," Myler said.

"So we will. Then we'll start crawling in even before it gets dark."

"They may not stay that long."

"They'll stay because this is the only road east from Getty's place. Those hills back there are the Texas line."

Myler said, "You're just guessing they'll stay."

Sundance said, "It's all guessing. Both of you, get some sleep and I'll keep watch. Don't guzzle all the water because you think there's water in that town. It may be dry as dust."

Sundance checked the hobbles on the horses before he watered them and settled down to watch the abandoned camp. It remained quiet; no activity of any kind. He could see the top of a bleached building with a livery sign. That's where their horses would be. They were eating cold food; no smoke showed. They might be together, or they might have taken up new positions. They were doing it pretty well, but that lamp had been a mistake. They should have hidden their horses a distance from town, hitched them securely, then come back and waited in ambush, in silence.

He hoped they could end it here in this snake-infested and deserted town. If they could just take one of them alive! He might not want to tell a straight story to Blaisdell, but he'd talk his head off when the pain became unbearable. Torture sickened Sundance, but sometimes torture was the only way to get at the truth. Later, he might try to change his story. That was all right: Blaisdell's word would carry more weight; they would have to let Myler go.

Myler and Blaisdell sweated in their sleep, their hats pulled low over their eyes, twitching and muttering as flies lighted on their faces. Sundance woke them and made them drink water and eat salt.

"Get the salt down and drink more water," he ordered.

"What time is it?" Myler asked, gagging on the rough salt. "God damn it, how much salt do we have to eat?"

"What I tell you to. Go back to sleep. I'll tell you when it's time."

Blaisdell stoppered his canteen. His face was streaked with sweat and he winked a dead fly from the corner of his eye. He rubbed at the stump of his arm, a habit he had. Maybe it still gave him pain after so many years.

"What are they doing now?" he asked.

"Nothing," Sundance said. "If they don't move on soon, they'll stay the night." He looked up at the sun, sailing across the sky like a glowing ball of brass. "They may not light the lamp again. We have to be in there before it gets dark. They may not be set up so early. I'm hoping they won't."

"We'll all be in the dark," Myler said. "The blind looking for the blind."

Sundance turned away to watch the town. "That's the idea," he said. "Let them come looking for us. We have prison shotguns and that gives us a big advantage in the dark."

Myler wasn't ready to believe anything. "What if *they* have shotguns?"

"Then it won't be so easy. Now shut up and go back to sleep. If you can't sleep, close your eyes and rest. Think of all the great things you're going to do when you get back to San Sebastian."

Myler said there was no way he could get back to sleep, but in a few moments he was snoring. Blaisdell remained awake, his hat over his eyes, and now and then he slapped at a fly.

Late in the afternoon, Sundance spotted a face at the open hay-hoist of the livery stable. It pulled back out of sight before he was able to adjust the screw of the binoculars. Maybe it was Ringelman. He couldn't be sure. He guessed two were asleep, one man on guard. Not being professionals, they must be getting edgy by now, for only the true killer knew how to wait without impatience. Men he knew and had known had the patience to lie all day under a blanket just to get one shot at some passing rider. He knew. He had done it himself. Killing was the greatest game of all; you figured out the moves you were going to make, always aware that the other man might have figured them out before you. It was a deadly game and some men lived only to play it.

He looked at the town, printing its images on his brain so there would be no false starts, no loss of direction when darkness came. He would start first, then wait for five minutes while the others followed. He guessed Myler and Blaisdell would do their best when the shooting started. They might not be good with guns; with shotguns that didn't matter so much; all you had to do was get close enough. Blaisdell, with one arm, would not be able to reload, so his first shots would have to count. If it came to a stand-off, Sundance would burn the town and drive them out in the open. But that was risky and he wouldn't do it unless he had to.

The sun was low over the western horizon when he told Blaisdell to prod Myler awake. "A few more minutes," he said. "Listen to me and listen good. Rub dust on your faces and when you follow, do it a little at a time. Keep your backsides down or they'll get shot off. No sudden movements that will catch somebody's eye. If you come across a snake, try to crawl away from it. Don't try to shoot it. You won't be fast enough and you'll get shot instead. I'll go first, then you wait five minutes before you start after me. If I get shot, leave me and get the hell away from here if you can. You won't be able to do me any good and you'll just get killed. Head back for Getty's place and hope to God you make it. Find the Mexicans watching the road and maybe they won't murder you. You got all that?"

"How could we not get it?" Myler said, long-faced. "You paint such a gruesome picture."

Sundance crawled through the brush with the shotgun cradled across his arms. A hundred yards out, he raised his head by inches, parting the brush with his fingers. Nothing stirred but brush and tumbleweed and wind-blown dust. He waited for the lamp to show light. It didn't. He thought he heard the whinnying of horses. He got closer and soon he was only fifty yards from the south end of the street. It was all but dark when he reached the end of the rotting boardwalk. He began to count off the minutes. Before he finished, he heard Myler and Blaisdell making more noise than they should have. No matter. They were all he had.

Nothing happened; there wasn't a sound. "They're in position," Sundance whispered. "They'll stay there if we don't pull them out."

"How?" Blaisdell asked, lying flat, the shotgun beside him.

"We have to find a place," Sundance answered. "We'll get set up and let them come looking."

Crouched low, they moved down the street in the dark, waiting for gunfire to erupt. There was a saloon with the swinging doors still in place. They creaked in the wind. "I'm going in," Sundance said. "If nothing happens, you come in after me."

Sundance crawled under the creaking doors and stood

up, bracing himself for bullets. None came. He felt his way to the bar and made his way to the end of it. His hand touched a candle stuck in the top of a bottle and he caught it before it fell to the floor. Myler and Blaisdell came in under the door.

"Maybe they're not here," Myler whispered.

"They're here," Sundance said. "Move back from where you are. I'm going to light the candle. Let them know we're here. Let them decide what to do about it."

The match flared in Sundance's hand, and their faces were sweaty black in the light. Sundance looked around the wrecked saloon; the mirror behind the bar was smashed, the floor inches deep in dust.

"What if they don't take the bait?" Myler whispered, twitching every time the batwing doors creaked. "They don't have to do anything."

Down the street a horse whinnied, then it was quiet again.

Chapter Thirteen

"THEY'LL come looking for us," Sundance said. "They'll come and we'll be waiting. We'll draw them in and maybe they'll give up their guns when they see what they're facing. For your sake we have to take them alive if we can."

Myler said, "You think that's possible, Sundance?"

"Probably not. They know they'll hang. They didn't just murder that man in the card game. They thought it out, fixed it so everything would fit. The courts don't like to be used to frame people—they know they'll hang if they're captured."

"Then why don't we ambush them and kill them?" Blaisdell said.

"You're forgetting about me," Myler said. "If there's one we don't have to kill, that's enough to clear me."

"Button your lip, Selden," Sundance ordered. "You're talking when we should be getting set. You watch the back door and Blaisdell will go up on the balcony and shoot from there. Take a shotgun, Blaisdell, and brace it against the wall behind you. The wall will take the kick, all right?"

"I can do it," Blaisdell said. "We should try to take at least one of them. You're doing it this way because you don't think we're good enough. I don't mean you, naturally."

"You don't mean me either," Myler snapped. "I don't want to be included with you!"

"Why don't you try and talk them to death?" Sundance said. "Take up your position and be quiet."

The candle fluttered in the wind and there was hardly a sound after Sundance went behind the bar and sat on a beer keg with the shotgun across his knees. He wondered how Myler and Blaisdell were going to hold up when the shooting started. The Actor, an amiable man, had more nerve than both of them. Sundance smiled when he thought of the Actor and all the roles he was going to play. What were some of them? Itinerant preacher, painless dentist with his tools in the pawnshop. Maybe the Actor was dead by now; there was a good chance of it.

He looked in the dusty mirror and wasn't able to see Blaisdell on the balcony. Myler was behind the wrecked player piano. According to Myler, the three men they were hunting—or being hunted by—were not professionals. But what did Myler know about killers of any kind? Myler said they looked and talked like small ranchers, but every killer was something else before he became a killer. The rebellious private soldier shot a bullying sergeant in the back and ran away and kept on killing. The resentful boy burned the house down around his mother and the man who wasn't Daddy in her bed. They all got their start in one way or another.

Waiting never made Sundance impatient, as it did other men, because every moment of waiting was another moment of life. There were arguments to the contrary, but he wasn't swayed by them.

A sudden snap of wind blew dust in the door and

down the street a loose board fell with a clatter. Myler jumped at the sound, causing the piano wires to vibrate. It might be a loose board, or it might have been thrown to get a reaction. Upstairs a floorboard creaked, but that could nothing more than the stresses of an old building.

The swinging doors shattered under the impact of a rock and a man dived in low, rolled away and came up holding a rifle. Sundance blew his head off with one barrel of the shotgun. Up on the balcony, Blaisdell turned the shotgun as a man came at him from behind. No longer braced against the wall, the twin blast of the shotgun knocked him down when he tripped both triggers at the same time. Sundance killed the attacker with the second barrel while he was pegging shots at Blaisdell. The blast struck him in the lower chest and belly and he screamed and pitched down the stairs and didn't move after he got there. There was a yell and the third man came through the door and tried to turn, his nerve gone. He would have thrown up his hands if Myler hadn't steadied his pistol on top of the piano and shot him in the side. He fell, clutching his side, begging for mercy before he shuddered and lay still. Myler ran at him with the pistol cocked for a second shot and he was aiming at the man's face when Sundance jumped over the bar and wrestled the gun away from him. Myler was twitching and smiling at the same time.

"Let me finish the bastard," he screamed. "Every day on that rockpile I could see these bastards' faces!"

Sundance shook him until he stopped shouting. "He's shot enough," he said. "If he lives you'll have a witness."

The three men lay in the sifted sand of the saloon floor. Only Ringelman was still alive, with blood leaking from his side, mixing with the sand. Woodruff had his head blown to bits, Haggard's belly was torn by buckshot. Myler beat his fist into his open palm as he stared down at them. "God damn it," he kept saying. "That last fellow is going to die, and I'm the one that shot him, God damn me!"

Sundance knew what he was thinking. "You still have Blaisdell's word that he saw what happened. That should be enough to clear you, Selden."

"How? By saying these men tried to kill us? We're in the middle of nowhere, Sundance. The bodies'll be rotted to stink and who's to say who these men were?"

"I'll say what they looked like," Blaisdell said, walking over to stare at their faces. "I'll do what I can, Myler."

"Selden's right," Sundance said, kneeling beside Ringelman, cutting away his shirt with the Bowie. "We have to keep this one alive." He inspected the wound. "Two ribs are broken and the bullet is still in there. He's losing too much blood. Pull some tables together and clean them off. Then see how much oil is left in the other lamps. You, Blaisdell, go in the kitchen and see if there's anything to boil water in. A tin basin, a pot."

Blaisdell shouted from the kitchen, "There's a pot."

"Get water from the canteens," Sundance said. "Take my skinning knife and hold the blade in the water till it boils. After that's done, tear your shirt in strips and boil them too. Infection will kill this man quicker than the bullet."

Myler was dusting off the tables with his hat. "I wanted to kill Ringelman. Now I'm praying he'll live."

"Pray hard and hold him when I start using the knife. Blaisdell can sit on his legs if he starts to come round. Help Blaisdell check the lamps."

Myler and Blaisdell went upstairs and came back with two hanging lamps. "There's just a trickle of kerosene," Blaisdell said, shaking the lamp. "How long will it take?"

"Till I get the bullet out," Sundance answered. "Go get the water if it's boiled."

Myler trimmed the wicks and lit the lamps and hung them over the tables. Then he cleaned the chimneys and put them in place. "Turn up the wicks," Sundance said. "I need more light. Hurry up with the water, Blaisdell."

Sundance told Myler to tilt one of the lamp shades as he picked up the knife from the steaming water. The knife was clean, his hands were clean. "Hold him," he said.

Ringelman groaned as the tip of the knife probed the wound. The blood was still coming and maybe an artery had been nicked. Feeling the knife point grate against a shattered rib, Sundance moved it and continued to probe. Ringelman opened his eyes just as the point of the knife touched the bullet and he roared like a wild man, not so much from pain as from panic.

"Stay still or you'll die," Sundance said. "Give him something to bite on, Selden."

Myler put a sliver of broken furniture between Ringelman's teeth.

The piece of wood snapped as Sundance worked the knife behind the bullet and began to bring it out. "He's out cold," Myler said, releasing his grip on Ringelman's shoulders. The bullet came out and Sundance dropped it on the floor. "Get the bandages in here, Blaisdell. Don't touch them. I'll squeeze them out. Sit him up when I tell you, but do it easy."

After the wound was bandaged they dragged a mattress downstairs and put Ringelman on it. "No blankets, they took all the blankets," Myler said.

"Wake up, Selden," Sundance said. "Get blankets from the horses. It's going to get cold soon. We'll know in a few hours if he's going to live. One of you make something to eat."

One of the lamps went out before the food was ready. "Open a can of condensed milk and spoon it into him," Sundance said. "No food yet."

They ate at a dusty table, haggard and gritty-eyed, but no longer tense. The other lamp died and they were left with the candle. Tumbleweed rasped along the front of the building and sand blew in the door.

"They had it set up nice," Myler said. "The first three men were just sent to hurry us along, wear us down for the kill. And all the time three more were waiting up ahead."

"I don't know," Sundance said, pouring another cup of coffee. "Looks like it. Maybe it wasn't that neat. One way or another, they went to a lot of trouble. I figure telegraphs went out all over as soon as the break was discovered. The three poker players were sent to finish the job they started in the saloon. You still don't know who they were?"

"Just ranch men passing through, is what they said they were. Strangers to one another, they said. They gave their right names because my lawyer checked back to see if they were tied to the Ring. They weren't."

"The Ring uses outsiders when it suits them," Sundance said. "These men must have been paid well to do what they did. The trial was over and you were in jail for life, no hope of escape. It must have rattled them when they heard you were out."

"I didn't rattle them, *you* did," Myler said.

"Whatever. They knew they had to act together because they were all part of the murder and would hang if the truth came out. If any of them ran, the others could give him away. They weren't professional gunmen, a good thing for us. Anyway, that's what I figure. We'll know for sure if Ringelman pulls through."

"What if he won't talk?" Myler asked, turning his head to look at the wounded man.

"He'll talk," Sundance said. "The knife can be used more ways than one."

There wasn't much light left in the candle when Ringelman woke up and asked for water. Ringelman's eyes jumped from one face to another as they gathered round the table. Myler held a canteen to his mouth and let him drink. The bandage was soaked in blood, but the bleeding had stopped.

"Where are—?" Ringelman asked, moving his head, trying to see.

"They're dead," Sundance said. "You have a chance to live—maybe. I'll keep you alive or let you die, depending on what you say. This man—" he nodded toward Blaisdell— "is the superintendent of the Sanderson Penitentiary. Tell him how you and the others framed Selden Myler into his jail. Tell it straight, Ringelman. It's the only thing between you and Kingdom Come."

Ringelman closed his eyes and shook his head. "I won't talk. If this man is the jailkeeper, let him arrest me. I told the truth at Myler's trial and I won't go back on it. You can't kill me with the jailkeeper here."

Sundance looked at Blaisdell. "That right, jailkeeper?"

"Do what you like," Blaisdell said. "If he dies, I'll say he died of his wounds. Just don't ask me to watch."

Myler laughed crazily. "The jailer has a weak stomach!"

Sundance drew his gun and put the muzzle to Ringelman's eye. "You can't hide by closing your eyes." He took the gun away from Ringelman's face and put it against his ribs, just above the top of the bandage. "In ten seconds I'll bust the rest of your ribs," he said. "Thirty seconds after that you'll bleed to death. What's it going to be?"

Ringelman was sweating hard. "You got no right to be doing this to me!" His voice was stronger. "It was Woodruff and Haggard talked me into it."

Sundance kept the gun where it was. "Go back to the beginning and start there. Woodruff and Haggard didn't cook this up. Who did?"

"I don't know. Honest, I don't. Haggard knew this man from years ago when his father was selling meat to some reservation. Haggard's father, not the other man's. Haggard said this man—he didn't say the name —wanted to get Myler put away for life. We all had small ranches east of here and kind of knew each other by sight. I mean, Haggard knew Woodruff and Woodruff knew me. We lived miles apart, nothing to link us together."

"Except murder," Myler interrupted.

Sundance warned him to shut up. "Get on with it, Ringelman. How much money did you get?"

"My end was five hundred," Ringelman said. "I figure the others got more. I didn't want to do it, but Woodruff said how could it go wrong? We all needed the money, me most of all. Had three bad years in a row, my wife sick and . . . ."

Sundance made a fist at Myler, warning him to keep quiet. "You murdered that man to frame Myler. Say it, Ringelman."

"We framed Myler," Ringelman repeated. "Haggard

shot the man and Woodruff knocked out Myler. Then they planted the hold-out cards so it would look like Myler was cheating."

"Did the murdered man accuse Myler of cheating?"

"No. He was a stranger that happened along."

"What was your part in it?"

"I doused the light." Ringelman's eyes begged Blaisdell for mercy. "You have to help me, sir. I was there but I didn't pull the trigger. Don't that make a difference?"

"Not a bit," Blaisdell said. "As soon as you're able to travel, I'm taking you back. Myler will be coming too. I don't know what the court will do with you. It's not up to me."

Weakened by talking, Ringelman drifted off into unconsciousness, but his pulse remained strong. "Looks like you've got yourself a prisoner," Sundance said.

"Two prisoners, if you count Myler."

"What about you?"

"I'm no kind of prisoner."

"Then you will remain a fugitive."

"Well, it won't be so bad. The men we killed together, you can't call that murder. Was killing Bracken murder?"

"No," Blaisdell said. "I'll tell the authorities you did it to save my life. Where will you go?"

"I'm not saying, Blaisdell. You might change your mind after you leave here and try to turn me in. Take your pick: Mexico, Canada, South America. A warning: don't change your mind about Myler, or I'll come looking for you."

Blaisdell looked surprised. "Of course I'll tell the truth. Why should I change my mind? As a prison official I am also an officer of the law."

"Also you're the strangest son of a bitch I ever met," Sundance said. "I don't know that a man like you should be allowed to live."

Blaisdell allowed himself a bleak smile. "You should have thought of that sooner. Now you need me and it's too late."

"You'll get yours, Blaisdell. Men like you always do."

"Yes, I suppose I will," Blaisdell said quietly.

Sundance shook hands with Myler and started for the door. "Give Ringelman a week and then start back," he said. "Tell the jailkeeper to go north to the railroad. You can ride back from there."

Myler followed him outside, waiting for something else. "What do I tell Crook?"

"Tell him I'll be in Juarez for a while," Sundance said. "If there is any good news, he can reach me there. If I can't come back, tell him thanks for everything. Goodbye, Selden. One last thing: for Christ's sake, will you stop calling the Indians 'my Indians'? It gets on my nerves!"

Juarez was right across the river, Rio Grande, from El Paso. To get there, Sundance crossed the border into Texas and rode south. If they were looking for him in Texas, he didn't see any signs of it. Taking it easy, he got to Mexico in two weeks.

He had passed through Juarez many times in years gone by. As a very young man he had been a soldier in the Army of the North when the *insurrectos* defeated the French-officered forces of Maximilian. The houses and churches of the sprawling border city still bore the scars of the fighting of thirteen years before. Now President Diaz ruled: the brown-faced Indian who wanted to be king.

Juarez, for all its noise and color, was not to Sundance's liking. One of the wildest towns in North America, it was the jumping-off place for all the would-be soldiers of fortune in the Southwest; all the runaway farm boys, gunmen, deserters and escaped convicts.

Sundance smiled at the thought. It was hard to think of himself as a fugitive jailbird, but that's what he was. Better get used to it. He knew he could have stayed in the States, gone far north and found a safe place in some remote mountain valley. He supposed he could stay there until civilization followed—or the law.

He had engineered an escape from a territorial prison, which meant that federal marshals would be looking for him. And the federal men weren't like the state or local law. They crossed state lines at will, they didn't give up. Too many people knew what he looked like; to pass himself off as other than he was—impossible.

He could go back to the Cheyenne, his mother's people, but even there he had old enemies and the question would be asked: why have you returned after so many years? If you are a hunted man, then why do you not seek help from your friend Three Stars? Or even worse, the hotheads might expect him to lead them in yet another war against the whites. No, he could not go back to the Cheyenne.

He had some money left, but when that was gone he would have to find work for his weapons. In Mexico there was no other work for a man like him. There were a dozen generals with private armies who would be pleased to make him an officer, for he knew guerrilla warfare as well as any man. Ever plagued by bandits, the American, British or German businessmen who owned the great ranches and mines and railroads of the

North were always looking for men skilled in the use of weapons. He could even get rich, if he stayed in Mexico.

But when he thought about money, he realized how unimportant it was to him. Let other men grub for it; he would not. There was no way he could help the Mexican Indians as he did those of the United States. Diaz could have done much for the Indians; instead, an Indian himself, he spurned his Indian blood and gave away the country to foreigners so he could stay in power. It was in their interest that he should retain an iron grip on the country. Diaz, the schemer, used Indian soldiers—most of the Mexican Army was made up of purebloods—to fight their own people.

Flawed though it was, the American government honored some agreements with the tribes. At other times, the men who governed, some of them, were brutal, hypocritical, and money-hungry. In the United States there were good men; the law was not publicly scorned, as it was in Mexico. So, to fight for the Indians in Mexico meant to lead open rebellion. It was no good, Sundance decided. All his life he had been an outsider, an outlaw who used the law when it could be used, and if an unjust law stood in his way, he tried to find a way around it, but only when there was no alternative. In the end, his own country—the country that didn't want him —was where he belonged.

He could stay in Juarez only so long. The hotel room he had was small and cleaner than the usual bordertown lodgings. It had a bed, a chair, a table, a cracked chamberpot. It was a place to sleep, and nothing more.

He would wait a month, and after that he would move on until he found some rancher or mine operator in trouble. As a rule, trouble meant bandits or rustler gangs. The work was dangerous, but the pay made up for it. And when the work was done, once again he would find someone else who wanted to hire his services.

Waiting bored him; it was hard to be patient. During the day he walked around the town, drinking bitter black coffee in places where his appearance caused no surprise. He stayed away from the cantinas where the American gunmen hung out, trying to make their drinks last through the day; loudmouths with fancy gun-rigs that fooled no one who was looking to recruit real men.

When he felt like it, he enjoyed a woman in a whorehouse he knew to be clean. He ate, he drank coffee, he slept. Two weeks passed, and his money was running low. Another week dragged by and he began to make preparations to leave. Then, with only one more day to go, a Mexican boy came to his room with a telegraph message. It was from Crook and it said:

>COME HOME ALL IS FORGIVEN SEE YOU
>IN DENVER—THREE STARS.

"Looks like you're off the hook," Crook told Sundance. "Blaisdell and Ringelman testified at Myler's new trial. More a hearing than a trial. Blaisdell by himself would have been enough. That's why Ringelman didn't try to change his story. A good thing for him he didn't—the judge was ready to send him to the gallows. I guess the prosecutor stuck a bargain. Ringelman got twenty years in the Cage."

"Then he'll be seeing plenty of Blaisdell," Sundance said. "Depends on which one dies first."

Crook shook his head and picked from an envelope from his desk. "Blaisdell's dead. After the trial, he went back to his hotel and put a bullet in his head. First, though, he made this statement and had it witnessed.

Tidy sort of a fellow. He said his statement was in the nature of a dying declaration. Legally, I don't know if that holds water. No matter. He admitted all the rotten conditions that prevailed in the Cage. The graft, the cruelty. He said he was finished as a man and a bullet was the only way out.''

"So he escaped, too."

"You could put it that way. He had a lot to say about you. Said you were all a man should be, all that he was not. Paid you a lot of compliments, Jim. How you saved his life and so forth. You want me to read it?"

"No thanks, Three Stars."

Crook shrugged and put the envelope in a drawer. "I took his statement to the governor and he hemmed and hawed about your law-breaking, but you got a full pardon just the same. If he suspected I was in on the jailbreak, he didn't say anything about it. But you're *not* to do it again. Me too, I guess. How was Mexico?"

"I was getting tired of it," Sundance said, smiling. "Any word on the prisoner who broke out with me?"

"Not a trace of him. Vanished from the face of the earth, it looks like. They tell me he poisoned his father."

"So he told me."

"You say that so casually."

"I wouldn't be here if not for Maitland—the Actor. Fifteen years in the Cage was enough to pay for two or three fathers. Fathers of the kind he described."

Crook gave a sour smile. "I wouldn't mind poisoning a few of my relatives."

Sundance smiled too. "You shouldn't hang around with jailbirds, Three Stars. You're beginning to sound like Myler. Is he back at San Sebastian?"

"No way the Indian Ring could block that," Crook

said. "I told him to hire a new assistant and let him do the work for a while. The doctor says he has bad lungs, but he has a chance if he takes it easy. Knowing Myler, I doubt it. That's his business."

"I still think about the Cage," Sundance said. "Is there any hope that things will change with Blaisdell gone? Come to think of it, Blaisdell would have made some changes."

Crook said, "The governor said he was going to make some changes himself. The governor is a politician and I had to twist his arm somewhat." Crook smiled. "That was after he signed your pardon and couldn't take it back. 'Governor,' I said. 'It would be a terrible thing if the newspapers—here, in Washington, all over—got hold of Blaisdell's statement.' That was when he asked if I had a copy and I said I just happened to have one locked away in a safe place. Both of us nodded wisely and he said it might be a good idea if I destroyed the copy. I said I'd probably get around to it."

"It's better than nothing, Three Stars."

"Don't expect miracles, Jim. At least Captain Tyson's gone from the prison service. God knows what he'll do next. Go to Brazil where they still have slavery. He'd be good as an overseer."

"Maybe I'll run into him some day," Sundance said. "I wouldn't mind that."

"Don't tell me about it," Crook said. "But I won't break down and cry if I hear about it. Might even send flowers—stinkweed. What are your plans, now that you're an honest citizen again?"

"Go away for a while," Sundance answered. "Far from men and the things they do. I get a bad feeling in my head if I don't do that. Then maybe I'll go and see

Myler. It's a long time since I've been to San Sebastian."

Crook raised his eyebrows in surprise. "Don't tell me you and Myler have become friends?"

"Hell, no, Three Stars! As they say, Myler isn't hard to like, he's impossible to like."

"Some people say the same thing about me."

"With good reason, Three Stars," Sundance said, returning Crook's smile. "You got anything to say to Myler if I run into him?"

"Damn right I have," Crook snorted. "Tell that damn fool to stay away from the card tables and all other games of chance."

Sundance got up to go. "You never took a chance in your life, did you, Three Stars?"

"Not me," Crook said. "I always bet on a sure thing. Now a fellow like you, you're not half as wise as I am." They shook hands. "See you soon, halfbreed—stay out of jail."

"I'll do my best," Sundance said.

SUNDANCE #40: THE HUNTERS
By Peter McCurtin

PRICE: $1.95 LB1010
CATEGORY: Western

SURVIVAL OF THE FITTEST

Manning, an English big-game hunter, hires Sundance to act as his guide hunting grizzlies in the mountains. What Manning really wants to do is hunt Sundance —a man-hunt, with the fittest surviving.

HELLTOWN
By Dallas Todd

PRICE: $1.95 LB1004
CATEGORY: Adult Western

DIRTY DOINGS IN BLACK CREEK!

George Cullane was just passing through the little town of Black Creek, when all hell broke loose. After a hotel fire interrupted his one-night stand with a red-hot lady, Cullane suspected arson, and decided to stick around long enough to find out who was behind it.

GOLD STRIKE
(SUNDANCE SERIES #35)
By Peter McCurtin

PRICE: $1.75   LB819
CATEGORY: Western

Jim Sundance came across one of the biggest gold strikes the Territory had ever known. Millionaire miner Jackson Selby wanted in on the halfbreed's action, but Sundance wouldn't sell. Soon, Sundance and a band of die-hard prospectors were dug in at the mine, ready for Selby's marauders. Death would determine the ownership of this gold mine!

BOUNTY HUNTER
By Aaron Fletcher
(AUTHOR OF OUTBACK)

PRICE: $1.75 LB1006
CATEGORY: Western

RIDING FOR REVENGE

The Civil War was over, but Jake Coulter's homecoming was not a happy one. His stepmother was dying, his father was dead, shot by two outlaws with a price on their heads. Only one thought burned in Coulter's brain—to avenge his family's death.

WARPAINT

By Les Wayne

PRICE: $2.25
0-8439-1042-9

CATEGORY: Western

Arvado Jones, a mountainman is still grieving over the loss of his Indian wife and son, when he encounters a group of travelers, two orphaned white children and a crazed old squaw. Fearing for their safety in hostile Indian territory, Arvado undertakes to guide his found "family." The squaw decides to invade the Cheyenne lodges, thinking she can find her dead husband, as Arvado comes to the rescue.

INDIAN TERRITORY

By David Everitt

PRICE: $2.25   0-8439-1041-0   **CATEGORY:** Western

After killing a man in a gambling brawl, Doc Holliday barely escaped being lynched by an angry mob. Together with his brave and clever woman, Kate Elder, he rode off from Fort Griffin, Texas, heading north for Kansas. The safety of a new life in Dodge City, however, lay miles ahead — beyond the dangerous Indian Territory.

Gunslammer

By Ralph Hayes

PRICE: $1.75 0-8439-1043-7   **CATEGORY:** Western

Crazy Jake and his crew were as evil as they were ugly — especially now, when greed was clawing their guts. The marshal, who knew where the entrance to the gold mine was but refused to tell, died a gruesome death. His deputy was next on the murder list. Then buffalo hunter O'Brien came along and suddenly the odds changed.

SEND TO: **LEISURE BOOKS**
P.O. Box 511, Murry Hill Station
New York, N.Y. 10156-0511

Please send the titles:

Quantity	Book Number	Price
_____	_____	_____
_____	_____	_____
_____	_____	_____
_____	_____	_____
_____	_____	_____

In the event we are out of stock on any of your selections, please list alternate titles below.

_____	_____	_____
_____	_____	_____
_____	_____	_____
_____	_____	_____

Postage/Handling _____

I enclose _____

FOR U.S. ORDERS, add 75¢ for the first book and 25¢ for each additional book to cover cost of postage and handling. Buy five or more copies and we will pay for shipping. Sorry, no C.O.D.'s.

FOR ORDERS SENT OUTSIDE THE U.S.A., add $1.00 for the first book and 50¢ for each additional book. PAY BY foreign draft or money order drawn on a U.S. bank, payable in U.S. ($) dollars.

☐ Please send me a free catalog.

NAME _____

(Please print)

ADDRESS _____

CITY _____ STATE _____ ZIP _____

Allow Four Weeks for Delivery